'You made use of me today,' Max began, his saturnine cast of feature very pronounced.

'I had no objection to acting as your minder at the party. I enjoyed that. But I did object to the sexual experiment afterwards. You were obviously proving something to yourself when you asked me to make love to you.'

Abby's eyes fell. 'I was with you all the way until—well, until the last bit.' She smiled wearily. 'Maybe now you can see why life is so much easier for me without a man in it.'

'I don't scare so easily,' he assured her, and got up to sit beside her. 'I like a challenge. And you, Abigail Green, are very definitely a challenge.'

Dear Reader

I quite often receive letters from readers asking me to write about characters featured in minor roles in my previous novels. In response to these, and also because her story was just asking to be told, this one features Abby, who first appeared as the teenage sister of Laura Green in A VENETIAN PASSION. I've returned to Italy for part of the setting, but whereas Laura found romance among the canals and beautiful buildings of Venice, Abby runs into her hero, almost literally, on a steep hillside road in Umbria.

Abby played a small, but very important part in A VENETIAN PASSION. Now, at twenty-five, she takes the starring role in AN ITALIAN ENGAGEMENT. I hope you enjoy reading about her as much as I enjoyed telling her story.

Best wishes

Catherine

AN ITALIAN ENGAGEMENT

BY
CATHERINE GEORGE

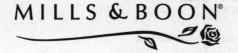

MILLS & BOON®

First published in Great Britain 2006
Harlequin Mills & Boon Limited,
Eton House, 18-24 Paradise Road, Richmond, Surrey TW9 1SR

© Catherine George 2006

ISBN-13: 978 0 263 84855 7
ISBN-10:   0 263 84855 8

Set in Times Roman 10½ on 12 pt
01-1006-54798

Printed and bound in Spain
by Litografia Rosés, S.A., Barcelona

AN ITALIAN
ENGAGEMENT

CHAPTER ONE

AFTER travelling the first stages by boat and train it was a relief to take to the road for the last lap of her journey. Abby checked the map, took a minute or two to familiarise herself with the hire car, then set off on a route which meandered through a sunlit Umbrian landscape with postcard views on all sides. But after a few kilometres the surface began to deteriorate. The road grew narrow and hair-raisingly steep, winding up in hairpin bends, each one tighter than the last. Abby crouched over the wheel, praying she wouldn't meet any oncoming traffic, her eyes too firmly glued to the road to notice the warning light on the dashboard. Suddenly a geyser of steam spurted up from the bonnet, a smell of hot metal filled the car, and a despairing look at the temperature gauge confirmed that it was almost off the clock.

Abby pulled over as far as she could against the hillside, yanked hard on the handbrake to secure the car on the steep incline, released the bonnet switch and got out, eyeing the car with hostility. It was obviously too hot to touch, but in the afternoon sunlight it was unlikely to cool down any time soon, either. Using a clump of tissues to protect her fingers, she raked up the bonnet and jumped back to avoid scalding jets of steam. The radiator obviously needed water more than she did. Great. Abby took her phone from her bag to explain why she was late. And ground her teeth in frustration. No signal. No choice, then, either. She had to walk. She reached in the car for her hat, then shot straight out again as she heard the roar of a powerful engine somewhere up ahead. Acting on instinct, she darted in front of her car, waving her hat in frantic warning as a flame-red vehicle came surging round the bend through a cloud of dust. Abby jumped out of the way at the last minute, her heart hammering at her ribs as the car swerved to halt just a yard or so away, its heavy tyres scattering shale and pebbles in all directions. Shaken and breathless, she stood her ground as six feet of furious male jumped out and bombarded her with a spate of Italian so rapid and incensed she could barely understand a word of it.

Knowing she'd only get another flood in response if she uttered a word of her own very basic Italian, Abby held up her hand like a traffic policeman, took off her dark glasses and smiled ruefully. 'I'm terribly sorry. My car's broken down. Do you speak English?'

The man's eyebrows shot up over aviator lenses. 'Good God. You're a Brit?'

'Yes,' she said, surprised, because so was he.

'What the devil are you doing here? I could have killed you! This is a private road.'

Her smile faded. 'I'm aware of that. I'm on my way to an appointment at the Villa Falcone.'

'Oh, right. Another of Gianni's fans,' he said, in a tone which raised her hackles.

She gave him a frosty look. 'My appointment with Mr Falcone is strictly business.'

'That's what they all say.' He thrust a hand through his hair, scowling at her. 'That was a damn stupid thing to do. Be grateful my brakes are efficient.'

Abby was used to dealing with people in her job, but she was hot, tired, late for an appointment, and in no mood for a lecture. 'If this road is Mr Falcone's private property are *you* a fan, or just a trespasser?'

'For your information,' he drawled, 'it's not Gianni's private road. It's mine.'

'Oh.' Abby's hot face reddened in embarrassment. 'Then I apologise. I must have taken a wrong turn somewhere.'

'Obviously. Let's take a look at your car.'

Abby raked the bonnet up again and stood back. He hooked his sunglasses in his belt and bent over the engine to investigate. She looked on without much hope, but when he straightened to wipe sweat from his forehead she frowned in surprise. The tanned, saturnine face looked familiar. She could have sworn she'd seen him before— Oh, come *on*, Abigail. How likely was that? Stress and heat were frying her brain.

'Your radiator's sprung a leak,' he informed her. 'A stone probably pierced it from underneath. You wouldn't have noticed on this surface. My apologies.'

Abby smiled graciously. 'Hardly your fault.'

'The apology is for my suspicions. I took it for granted the breakdown was staged.' His smile set her teeth on edge. 'Gianni's fans can be amazingly creative in their attempts to get at him.'

She needed this man's help, she reminded herself. 'I assure you that Mr Falcone is expecting me.' She looked at her watch in dismay. 'In fact I'm due to meet him in twenty minutes, but I can't get a signal to tell him I'm delayed.'

'You won't in this spot. I'll drive you back to my place to ring Gianni. He can send someone to pick you up.' A pair of hard, deep-set eyes gave her a look she didn't care for very much. 'Were you expecting to stay at his house overnight?'

'No,' she said coolly. 'I'm booked in at a hotel in Todi. After my meeting with Mr Falcone I'll get back there by taxi.'

For the first time he gave her a genuine, megawatt smile. 'Right, let's go, then. My name's Wingate, by the way.'

'Abigail Green,' she said, dazzled by the smile. 'I appreciate your help, Mr Wingate.' She collected her belongings from the car and locked it, wiped her hands on a tissue, jammed her panama low on her forehead and got into the passenger seat of what she could now see was a Range Rover sports car. The perforated leather of the passenger seat supported her in pure comfort after the cramped little hire car, but Abby sat rigid, eyes firmly averted from the drops below, while her reluctant Samaritan turned the car in a skilled, terrifying manoeuvre, then took off up bends which grew more hair-raising the higher they climbed. At last, to her infinite relief, they passed through a gap in weathered walls into the courtyard of a house built of pale, sun-washed stone.

'Oh, how lovely,' she said involuntarily. The infrequent windows were of different sizes and set in the walls with no apparent eye for symmetry, but the effect was utterly captivating. When she got out she could see that each window had been placed to look down on a different view of wooded hills and vineyards, interspersed with cultivated fields protected by serpentine rows of tall cypresses.

'What a fantastic panorama,' she said, impressed. 'It's almost worth the drive up here to look down at it.'

'Not many people agree with you on that—fortunately.' He ushered her into the house through a porch with greenery twining round its pillars. 'Come inside out of the sun.'

Abby followed him across a cool hall to a living room with exposed beams and massive stone fireplace.

'Sit down,' he invited. 'I'll fetch you some fruit juice.'

'Thank you.' She smiled a little. 'But I've been sitting all day, one way and another. Would you mind if I just stand at the windows to look at the view?'

The hard eyes softened as he gave her the smile again. 'Feel free. Where did you hire the car?'

'The hotel arranged it—the Villaluisa.'

'Right. I'll ring them after I get hold of Gianni.'

Alone with the view, Abby could hear him talking in rapid-fire Italian in another room, presumably with Giancarlo Falcone. She fervently hoped so. Otherwise she'd come a long way for nothing. When she'd begged time off to fly to Venice to meet her brand-new nephew, her boss had agreed as long as she made a detour to Todi on the way back to finalise details for the young tenor's first British concerts.

'Arrangements made,' said her host, returning with a tray. He poured fruit juice into a tall, ice-filled glass and handed it over. 'I'll drive you to the Villa Falcone myself.'

Surprised, Abby thanked him and drank thirstily. 'That's extremely kind of you,' she said after a moment. 'But I must be holding you up. You were on your way somewhere earlier.'

'I cancelled.' He raised an eyebrow. 'Is someone waiting for you at the hotel?'

She shook her head. 'I'm flying home tomorrow to get back to work on Monday. Thank you,' she added as he refilled her glass.

'What do you do?'

Abby gave him a brief description of her job as assistant to an impresario. 'I help organise various events. In summer it's mostly open-air picnic concerts in picturesque venues. A major part of my job involves looking after the performers, which is why I'm here right now. Giancarlo Falcone is a big draw, but he's been hard to pin down to an actual date, and brochure deadlines are looming.'

'So your boss thought the feminine touch would bring him to heel?'

'Only because I happened to be travelling to Venice to see my new nephew. My sister's husband is in the hotel business there.'

'He's Italian?'

She smiled a little. 'I think Domenico looks on himself as Venetian.'

'Then he must be elated to have a son.'

'He was, once he was sure that all was well with Laura. But he's equally besotted with the daughter who arrived first, two years ago.'

'You like children?'

'Of course.' Abby drained her glass. 'May I tidy up before we go?'

She took her bag into the cool marble interior of her host's ground-floor bathroom, wishing that her blue chambray shirt dress had survived her adventure rather better. She smoothed it down as best she could, unloosened the plaited leather belt a notch to lie lower on her hips, and went to work on her face with soap and water, followed by some copious moisturiser and her emergency supply of cosmetics. She used a scent spray sparingly, unfastened the denim barrette at the nape of her neck, brushed her hair out to curl loosely on her shoulders, then grinned cheerfully at her reflection. If the singer needed persuasion, it was only common sense to use whatever ammunition she had on hand to get him to sign.

Her rescuer was waiting for her in the cool, high-ceilinged hall, looking dauntingly immaculate now in a handkerchief-thin white shirt, beautifully tailored cotton trousers, and a leather belt and shoes obviously bought somewhere in Italy. And, she noted, he'd taken time to shave.

'I was right,' he said, studying her. 'One look at you and Gianni will be toast.'

'Good, if that means he'll sign,' said Abby serenely.

The hard eyes narrowed. 'Be careful, Miss Green. Gianni may sing like an angel, but he's as human as any other man.'

'I'm always careful,' she assured him.

'Not today. You took a wrong turning somewhere.'

'I won't do it again on that road,' she said with feeling.

'Pity.'

She raised an eyebrow. 'I thought you objected to trespassers.'

He gave her a direct look as he helped her into the passenger seat. 'In your case I'll gladly make an exception. And don't worry about the car. The hotel manager will send someone to collect it.'

'Thank you, Mr Wingate. You're very kind,' she added stiffly as they left the shelter of the walls for the road.

His lips twitched. 'You just happened to catch me in a good mood today.'

'It wasn't so good when we first met.'

He threw her a wry glance. 'I was bloody terrified! You do realise I could have killed you?'

'I do now.' She shrugged. 'But I just had to stop you somehow.'

'And stopped my heart while you were at it, when you jumped in front of me, waving that absurd hat! By the way,' he added casually, 'when you've sorted things with Gianni don't bother about a taxi. I'll drive you to Todi myself.'

Abby stared at him in surprise. 'I can't possibly trouble you to do that, Mr Wingate.'

'Of course you can. And the name's Max,' he added. 'Do I call you Abigail?'

'I prefer Abby.' She sat, white-knuckled, while he inched the Range Rover past the abandoned hire car. 'What made you build a house in a location like this?' she asked when she could breathe again. 'It needs nerves of steel just to get to it.'

'There's an easier road at the back of the property. My cleaner Renata goes up that way on her bicycle.'

'So why don't *you* use it?'

'I do sometimes, but it leads in the opposite direction from the Villa Falcone and Todi so it was back to the scenic route for this trip.' He shot her a glance. 'I didn't choose the location, by the way. I was given the property as a gift when I was a budding architect.'

Abby began to relax as the road levelled out into the leisurely winding route she'd found so pleasant earlier on. 'Did you become a full-blown architect?' she asked politely.

'Eventually, yes. This must be where you went wrong,' he added as they turned off on another road. 'Coming from Todi, you should have taken a right at this point.'

'A really stupid mistake,' she said in disgust. 'This would have been a much easier drive.'

'But then we might never have met,' he pointed out.

Not sure how to take that, Abby focussed her attention on the road winding up ahead through a grove of chestnut trees. Max Wingate halted at gates set between high stone walls, spoke into a microphone in one of the pillars, then drove up through formal gardens towards a house much older and bigger than his own hilltop retreat. Venetian windows, rose-coloured walls and an arcaded loggia were exactly how Abby pictured an Italian villa.

A familiar figure came hurrying out to greet them, smiling broadly.

'*Benvenuto; com' estai, Massimo?*'

'I'm good, Gianni. Speak English. This is Miss Abigail Green, all the way from England just to see you.'

Giancarlo Falcone was familiar to Abby from his publicity stills, but in the handsome flesh his looks had far greater impact. He had so far avoided the excess weight of many of his profession, and in black T-shirt and jeans he looked more like a sexy rock star than an operatic tenor. He bent over Abby's hand, his eyes bright with open appreciation as he straightened to smile at her. 'Welcome to my home, Miss Green.'

She returned the smile warmly. 'Thank you. I'm so sorry I'm late. My car broke down.'

'*Che peccato*! It is lucky that Max was on hand to rescue you.'

'Very lucky,' she agreed thoughtfully, looking from one man to the other. Max Wingate was several inches taller, and his thick sleek hair and eyes were the dark brown of bitter chocolate. Gianni Falcone's brilliant eyes and mane of waving hair were true Mediterranean black, but olive skin, aquiline features and slanting eyebrows were a common denominator on both faces. The resemblance was unmistakable.

'You've guessed our dark secret,' said Max, resigned.

'Secret?' queried Gianni.

'I neglected to mention that we're related.'

The singer's smile flashed white, his eyes dancing as he shook his head in mock sorrow. 'So. I am the skeleton in the cupboard. Max is ashamed of his little brother, Miss Green.'

'Half-brother,' corrected Max. 'Is Luisa here, by the way?'

'No.' Gianni gave him a wry look. 'Mamma is at home in Venezia.'

To Abby's surprise Max visibly relaxed. 'Oddly enough your visitor has travelled here from Venice today,' he told his brother.

'You were there on holiday, Miss Green?' asked Gianni.

'A very brief one,' she said, smiling. 'A flying visit to meet my brand-new nephew.'

'Ah, a joyous event—my felicitations.' He took Abby by the hand. 'Come. Let us go to the music room. Do you come too?' he asked his brother.

Max shook his head. 'I'll chat with Rosa in the kitchen while you get down to business, then I'll drive Miss Green to Todi afterwards.'

Gianni's eyebrows rose. 'I could have done that.'

Max snorted. 'No, you couldn't. If you set foot anywhere near the place you cause a riot these days. Abby's been travelling all day. She needs a peaceful evening.'

The emphasis in his voice brought an unholy gleam to his brother's eyes.

'Va bene—I understand. Perfectly! We shall be a few moments only while I sign whatever Miss Abby wishes me to sign. *Allora*,' he added, taking Abby's arm to lead her away. 'You shall have some tea to drink while we do this.' He glanced over his shoulder. 'Ask Rosa to bring it, Max, *per favore*, and for you whatever you wish.'

Gianni Falcone showed his visitor into a vast, high-ceilinged room dominated by a grand piano with an open opera score propped on it.

'I thought your agent would be here today, Signor Falcone,' said Abby, taking a contract from her bag.

'Gianni, please!' He shrugged. 'Luigi has already settled the terms with Signor Hadley. We do not need to bring him back from holiday just for the signing. I am happy to sing at two concerts next June as requested.' He gave her the megawatt smile familiar from his publicity stills. 'You will be there?'

'Yes, I'll be there,' she assured him, and gave him details of the hotel and travel arrangements she would arrange for him.

'I trust your choice, Miss Abby. And because it means we shall meet again I look forward to the concerts with much pleasure.'

'I notice you're working on Puccini's *Bohème*,' commented Abby. 'It's a favourite of mine.'

The black eyes gave her a melting look. 'Then I shall sing an aria from it just for you.'

While Gianni was reading through the contract, his brother came in with a tray, followed by a small woman carrying a coffee pot.

'I decided to join you for tea,' said Max.

Gianni looked up with a smile. '*Bene*. You are just in time to witness my signature—ah, Rosa *mia*, you have brought coffee just for me.'

The small plump woman smiled at him fondly, and said something rapid in Italian as she left.

'She's been with him since he was born,' Max informed Abby. 'She knows what he wants before he asks for it.'

'This is true,' admitted Gianni. He gave his brother a sly smile. 'But when I go to sing in London this lovely lady says *she* will look after me.'

Max shot a look at Abby. 'Is that part of the service?'

She nodded briskly. 'It's my job. I look after all the artists.'

Abby spent a very interesting half-hour with the two men, who, though related by blood, were so different otherwise they might have been from a different species. Gianni Falcone was outgoing and charming and all Latin. In contrast the saturnine good looks of his self-contained brother were very British, but Max Wingate made it so clear he was no more immune to her charms than his brother that Abby was sorry when it was time to leave.

Gianni presented her with a compact disc of operatic arias as he walked with them to the car. 'It is my latest recording, with my compliments,' he told her, then kissed her on both cheeks and held the passenger door open as he teased his brother about the brand-new Range Rover.

'Vesuvius orange—a hot colour but a very cool car, Max. He has a great weakness for cars, you understand,' he informed Abby.

His brother hooted in derision. 'How about that flash toy of yours?'

'My Lamborghini is not flash. It is *bellissima*!' Gianni embraced him affectionately and stood back. 'I shall see you in London, Miss Abby. You I will see sooner, Max. *Arrivederci*.'

'I was right,' said Max with satisfaction as the gates closed behind them. 'One look at you and Gianni was putty in your pretty little hands.'

Abby's eyes flashed as she thanked him punctiliously for driving her to the Villa Falcone.

He chuckled. 'That's not what you really wanted to say!'

She smiled reluctantly. 'True. But if I spoke my mind all the time I wouldn't last long in my job.'

'You find the artistic temperament tricky to deal with sometimes?'

'So far there's been nothing I can't handle, mainly because I do my research in advance.' She eyed him questioningly. 'The glorious voice apart, I don't know much about your brother.'

Max shrugged. 'Gianni's got his feet firmly on the ground. He enjoys the adulation and the fuss women make over him, but he won't give you any trouble.'

'You're obviously fond of him.'

'It's hard not to be fond of Gianni.' He gave her a sidelong glance as Todi rose into view on its hill. 'We're almost there. So, Miss Abigail Green, now you've got the business part over, let me show you something of the city tonight. I'll introduce you to some local cuisine afterwards.'

Abby stared at him in surprise. She had expected him to drop her at the hotel and take to his heels in relief, his rescue mission over. But she was utterly delighted by the idea. A meal alone in her room was no competition for dinner in Todi with a man like Max Wingate. 'Thank you, I'd love to see something of the town.'

He smiled. 'Good. Afterwards we can eat formally at the Ristorante Umbria, or more casually over pasta at the Cavour. Your choice.'

'Casual, please,' said Abby promptly. 'But I'll need half an hour to change.'

'I'll wait for you in the bar. Give me your car keys. I'll hand them over to the manager.'

Max watched her hurry away before he sought out the manager. He chatted with him for a while, and then settled at the bar with a glass of beer, prepared to wait a lot longer than half an hour. Not that he minded. Abigail Green was worth waiting for. When a frantic female had materialised in front of him on a road where he normally never saw a soul, he'd played hell with her from pure fright, because he could so

easily have killed her. Then he'd taken a good look at her and
thanked God his tirade had been in Italian. If she'd understood
a word of it he'd have had fat chance of persuading her to
spend the evening with him. And just the short time he'd
spent in her company so far had whetted his appetite for more.

The room Domenico had arranged for Abby looked out over
the hotel gardens and swimming pool, but for the moment her
interest was centred solely on the bathroom. She showered at
top speed, and to save time made brief phone calls to her
mother and Laura while she dried her hair and did her face. At
last, in a sleeveless black dress as simple as a T-shirt, she hung
long amber drops in her ears and went downstairs, prepared to
enjoy her evening out in Todi with a man who attracted her far
more than any man she'd met in a long time. If ever.

Max walked into the foyer just as Abby appeared, and
gave a heartfelt vote of thanks to fate as he smiled down at
the glowing face framed in a glossy fall of hair almost as dark
as his brother's. 'A woman of her word,' he commented,
tapping his watch. 'Dead on time. Are you still up for a stroll
before dinner?'

'I'm looking forward to it,' Abby assured him. 'My brother-
in-law says it's a very interesting city.'

'He's right.' Seized by an overpowering need to touch her,
he put a hand under her elbow as they walked to the car, wondering if she felt anything like the same jolt of heat as her bare
skin came in contact with his fingers. 'Todi's big on walls,
three concentric rings of them—medieval, Etruscan and
Roman, with some magnificent ancient gates. But the Rome
jet-set is fast catching up with Todi. Some of its medieval
houses have been restored as weekend getaways.'

'Your brother didn't fancy one of those?'

He shook his head. 'Gianni inherited the Villa Falcone
from his father, complete with Rosa and her crew to look after

him when he's home from his travels. And when his presence
is demanded in Venice he enjoys more pampering there from
his *mamma.*' He gave an approving glance at her flat gold
sandals. 'The streets are mostly cobbled, but I see you're
prepared for it.'

She nodded with enthusiasm. 'The only part of Italy I've
visited before is Venice.'

He smiled down at her as he held the car door open. 'You'll
enjoy the contrast. We'll park near the Piazza Oberdan. From
there it's a short climb to the church of San Fortunato and the
best view of the city.'

Abby's day had started early in Venice, with a ride by
water taxi followed by several hours by rail before the ill-fated
drive from Todi. But all that seemed a long way behind her
as she explored the ancient, beautiful city with Max Wingate.
The pace of life there seemed so much slower that Abby could
literally feel herself unwinding as they came down from San
Fortunato to wander through streets which Max told her had
changed little in appearance or purpose for centuries. They
looked at so much beautiful architecture as they strolled that
by the time they reached the basilica in the Piazza del Populo
Abby's action-packed day had caught up with her and she
agreed gratefully when Max suggested they walk down the
Corso Cavour in search of dinner.

'For your information, Todi's medieval piazza is one of the
most famous in Italy,' he told her as they reached the restaurant.

'I can well believe it. Todi's a delightful place. I only wish
I could stay here longer,' she said with a sigh.

'Come back when you have more time.'

'I'd certainly like to,' she said to be polite, but knew that
it was unlikely. Any trips to Italy meant Venice and a stay with
Laura, Domenico and Isabella. Plus the new baby.

'Your eyes lit up like lamps just then,' commented Max as
they were shown to a table beside a screen of greenery.

'What—or who—were you thinking about?' He hoped like hell it wasn't some man.

'Marco, my nephew, and his sister Isabella,' said Abby, smiling. 'It was hard to tear myself away from them this morning.'

'The only baby I've ever had much to do with was Gianni. But I was ten when he was born, and resented him pretty fiercely at the time. What sort of wine do you like?' Max added as a waiter handed out menus.

'Something dry and white, please—and some mineral water on the side.' Abby smiled crookedly as the waiter hurried off. 'This afternoon, stranded on your terrifying road, Mr Wingate, I would have sold my soul for water—for me *and* the car.'

His mouth tightened. 'In the circumstances it's lucky I'd arranged to play chess with Aldo Zanini. What the hell would you have done if I hadn't turned up?'

A chess game, then, not a date with some local *signorina*. Taken aback by how much that pleased her, Abby shrugged. 'Not much choice. I would have hiked—or climbed—the rest of the way. I had no idea I was on the wrong road, remember. What would *you* have done if I'd collapsed at your door, gasping for water?'

'Counted my blessings,' he assured her, giving her that smile again. 'Other than Renata on her bicycle, no woman ever makes it up to my place. But you're welcome any time, Abigail Green.'

The smile faded to something which made her pulse race as the dark eyes held hers, then the waiter arrived with wine and Max turned back to the menu. 'What would you like to eat? They do a good *tagliatelle al tartufo* here—pasta with truffles.'

'Sounds wonderful,' she said promptly. 'Though I'd probably fancy anything they cared to put in front of me—I had to skip lunch.'

'Truffle pasta for two, then.'

After some olives and a mouthful of cold dry wine Abby felt considerably better, and settled down to enjoy the kind of evening which rarely came her way during the summer season. 'So, Mr Wingate. When you're not on retreat in your eagle's nest where do you live?'

'In Gloucestershire, in a town called Pennington. I own a house within walking distance of my office building—why the smile?'

She chuckled. 'Would you believe I went to school in Pennington? I was brought up not far away from there in Stavely.'

Max shook his head in wonder. 'So you're a girl from the Shires—small world. But you're obviously based in London now.'

'And run home to Stavely every chance I get! You told me you're an architect, but what kind of work does your firm do?' asked Abby.

'We design large-scale buildings, mainly, but we also do individual work for people with specific requirements, like a recent client left partially paralysed after a road accident. I worked with him to modify his house, and now he can cope with everything in it from his wheelchair.'

'That must be a very satisfying thing to do,' she said, impressed.

'It is.' He smiled wryly. 'But I also do an increasing amount for clients brave—or mad—enough to invest in romantic ruins. My house out here is a good advertisement,' he said, topping up her glass. 'What led you into your kind of work?'

She shrugged. 'Fate, I suppose—coupled with a love of music. I read English at university, took a further business studies course after that, and while I applied for jobs I worked at the local stately home.'

'Do they get many graduates on their staff?'

Abby nodded. 'Quite a few in summer. But I had a foot in the door because I'd worked there before in vacations. The summer I graduated I helped out with a series of open-air concerts at the house, and got on very well with Simon Hadley, the events organiser. His permanent assistant left to have a baby before the end of the season and to my surprise he asked if I'd like the job. But after four seasons I feel it's time to move on. I finish in a couple of weeks.'

He eyed her narrowly. 'I thought you promised to see Gianni next summer!'

She flushed. 'I will see him. I'll be there at the concerts, but someone else will take care of him.'

Max shook his head in mock reproof. 'You mean you strung him along to make him sign on the dotted line.'

'I was acting under instructions from Simon,' she said firmly. 'But I wasn't lying. I'll definitely be in the audience when he sings.'

'But you won't be Gianni's nursemaid.' He leaned nearer. 'How do you know I won't betray your secret?'

She met his eyes squarely. 'I don't. Will you?'

He shook his head. 'I shall leave my little brother in blissful ignorance.'

'Thank you.' Abby sniffed rapturously as her truffle pasta was set before her. *'Grazie,'* she said to the waiter with a warm smile. *'Delizioso!'*

'The lad's gone off in a daze,' said Max, after the waiter had provided them with everything he could think of. 'He thinks you're *delizioso* too.'

'Rather sweet, isn't he?'

'I didn't notice. Eat. You can give me the rest of the Abigail Green life story afterwards.'

'Only if you tell me Max Wingate's in return,' she retorted, and smiled very deliberately into his eyes. 'Or should I call you "Massimo"?'

CHAPTER TWO

'GIANNI'S little joke,' Max said, resigned. 'My mother insists on calling me that because it was her father's name, but legally, and to everyone else, I'm Max.'

The waiter interrupted them to refill glasses with wine, but after a word from Max he left them in peace.

'I don't know what you said, but the poor boy looked really hurt,' said Abby reproachfully.

Max shrugged, unrepentant. 'Don't worry—the "poor boy" will be back the minute you swallow your last mouthful.'

She laughed, and went on with her meal with concentration which amused her companion. She set down her fork at last with a sigh. 'That was wonderful.'

'How about dessert?' said Max, rolling his eyes as the waiter hurried to their table.

'No room,' she said, trying not to laugh.

'Then it's back to your hotel. Unless you fancy another stroll around town?'

'It's certainly a delightful place,' she said obliquely, wishing now that she'd agreed to dessert if it meant more time with Max Wingate. Did she like him that much, then? Who was she kidding? Of course she did! Once he'd simmered down after the fright she'd given him he'd gone out of his way to help a stranger who'd not only disrupted his day but who had also almost given him a heart attack in the process. Gianni oozed natural charm, but Max's hard-edged persona appealed to her far more. There was something compelling about the dark, heavy-lidded eyes which gave her a shivery feeling every time they met hers.

'What are you thinking about?' he asked, so softly she had to crane to hear him above the noise and bustle of the restaurant.

Abby felt her face grow hot. 'Just how kind and helpful you've been.'

He leaned nearer. 'Don't endow me with non-existent virtues! I was kind as a means to an end—to coax you to spend the evening with me.'

She eyed him quizzically. 'Because you had to cancel your chess game?'

He shook his head. 'Aldo's the builder who worked with me on the house. I can play chess with him any time. When fate sent you up my road instead of Gianni's only a fool would have passed up the chance to take advantage of it. And I may be many things, but I'm no fool, Abigail Green.'

'I believe you!'

He sat back, studying her. 'Do you get much hassle from the male celebrities you deal with?'

'Sometimes it's a bit tricky with the ones who forget they're married, but nothing I can't handle with tact—so far.' Abby looked up with a smile for the waiter as he brought their espressos. 'Generally I get on well with men.'

'So I see!'

'I meant the men I meet professionally. And the ones in college, too. Before that, in school, all my friends were girls. I was a real turn-off for the boys at that stage—too skinny, too tall and too much of a swot.' She smiled philosophically. 'But by the time I went up to Cambridge to university I'd filled out a bit, everyone else was clever—a lot of them much more than me—and my social life took off into the fast lane.'

'I can well believe that!' He got up, and held out his hand. 'So, Miss Green. If you've finished your coffee and you can tear yourself away from our attentive waiter, let's rejoin the evening *passeggiata* for a while.'

Under a full moon the city looked more romantic than ever. Warning her to beware of uneven cobbles in some of the darker streets, Max took Abby's hand in his as they made a leisurely tour of some of the restored medieval houses, and after a while suggested they observe local custom and make for the *gelateria* across the park, to sample the local ice cream. 'It's very good—they make it with fresh fruit.'

'I'm still full of that fabulous meal,' Abby said with regret. 'Could we just wander round a bit more instead?'

'Anything you want,' he assured her, surprised to find he meant it quite literally. It was a long time since he'd walked anywhere hand in hand with a girl, and never with one who appealed to him as much as Abigail Green. 'Poor Gianni. This pastime is a simple pleasure he can't enjoy any more in his home town—one of the downsides to celebrity.'

'He must have a girlfriend, surely?'

Max nodded. 'But so far he's managed to keep her identity secret—even from his mother. Lord knows how. She thinks he tells her everything. Gianni confided in me because he was bursting to tell someone, but he wouldn't give me a name— probably because she's someone Luisa wouldn't approve of.'

'In what way?'

He shrugged. 'In his mother's eyes no woman in the world is good enough for Giancarlo Falcone.'

Abby eyed the aquiline profile curiously. 'He calls her Mamma. You don't.'

'If you met her you wouldn't believe she's old enough to be Gianni's mother, let alone mine.' He smiled down at her. 'How about you? What about your parents?'

'My father died when I was little, so my mother brought

us up almost single-handed. She's due in Venice next week to meet her baby grandson.' Abby smiled affectionately. 'Mother thought it only right to let his Italian grandparents get their visit in first. They own a restored farmhouse not far from here. Laura and Domenico spent their honeymoon there.'

'The ideal place for it.' Max halted as clocks began chiming. 'Alas, the witching hour. Time to get back to the car.'

Abby smiled warmly at him as they walked. 'Thank you so much for dinner and the fascinating tour of Todi. I enjoyed every minute of it.'

His hand tightened on hers. 'A pity you're not staying longer so I could persuade you to do it all again.'

'Perhaps you'll come to one of the concerts in London before I finish.'

He shook his head. 'If I do you'll be too busy to spend time with me. How about dinner with me one night instead?'

Abby saw no point in being coy. 'I'd like that very much.'

'In that case—' Max broke off as his phone rang. With a word of apology he listened for a moment before answering in fluent, irritable Italian. The heated conversation went on at length while he helped Abby into the car. When he finally slid into the driver's seat Max gave her a wry smile. 'My apologies. That was Gianni in full flow.'

'Something wrong?'

'As far as he's concerned total disaster. Luisa's taken it into her head to make a surprise visit to the Villa Falcone. She's ordered Gianni to meet her off the train in Perugia tomorrow.'

'He's not happy with that?'

'He's devastated. She's interrupting his idyll with the mystery lady.'

'Ah! So was he asking you to fetch your mother instead?'

'Practically begging. He's desperate to spend every minute he can with the love of his life, so he implored me to help him out. If I fetch his mother from Perugia tomorrow afternoon he can spend a few extra hours with his *innamorata*.' A smile played at the corners of his mouth. 'I said I'll ring him back to give my answer.'

'So will you help him?'

'I told him I had to sort something out first. You're travelling by train to Pisa tomorrow for the flight to London?'

'Yes,' said Abby cautiously.

'Then here's the plan. I drive you to Perugia, and see you off on the train to Pisa before I meet the one from Venice.' Max paused to gauge her reaction. 'Afterwards I drive back to the Villa Falcone at a snail's pace which, for entirely different reasons, will please both Luisa and Gianni. And somewhere along the way I'll ring him with an ETA so he can pursue love's young dream to the last possible moment.' He grinned. 'His *mamma's* coming to make sure he gets enough sleep before the Rome engagement, with no idea that he wants to do his sleeping with Signorina X.'

Abby chuckled. 'Oh, bad luck, Gianni! Are you willing to do that for him?'

'Yes. What do you say? It's one train connection less for you.'

'Then I'll say thank you very much indeed.' She eyed him curiously. 'Wouldn't it be quicker for your mother to fly?'

He shrugged. 'She won't. She refuses to travel by road, either, if she can help it, which is why Enzo, my stepfather, bought the apartment in Venice. Water taxis and trains are Luisa's preferred mode of travel. She'll get a surprise when I turn up as chauffeur,' he added. 'She doesn't even know I'm in the country.'

Abby was silent as they reached the hotel.

'Penny for them?' he said, turning to her.

'I was just thinking that it's very kind of you to drive me to Perugia tomorrow.'

His eyes locked on hers. 'If it weren't for Gianni and his love-life I'd drive you all the way to Pisa.'

Abby felt a lurch somewhere in the region of her midriff. 'Just to Perugia will be a great help,' she assured him.

'In that case I'll ring Gianni and tell him it's on.' Max began another rapid conversation with his brother, grinning broadly when he disconnected. 'Gianni practically burst into song with gratitude.'

'Will you take your mother up to your house first, to give him extra time with his lady?'

'No. According to Luisa the journey there is bad for her heart.'

Abby chuckled. 'I see her point, and there's nothing wrong with my heart! I must go in,' she added regretfully. 'The train from Perugia leaves at eleven fifty-two, according to my timetable. What time will you pick me up?'

'Ten sharp.'

'Perfect. I can have a leisurely breakfast instead of rushing off to catch the local train. Thank you—again,' she added, and smiled. 'I seem to have said nothing else to you from the moment we met.'

'Not quite,' he said, and took her hand. 'When I mistook you for one of Gianni's fans you were ready to punch me.'

'But I am a fan. I merely objected to the way you said it. Besides,' she added, eyes kindling, 'I'd just driven up those terrifying bends—on the wrong side of the road for me, remember—then the car broke down, and as the last straw this ball of flame came bursting out of the dust like something from an action film. I was petrified.'

'So was I.' He turned to look at her. 'But once I could breathe normally again I realised I'd run into the best-looking damsel in distress a man could hope to meet.'

She eyed him narrowly. 'I'm not sure if that's a compliment or a sexist remark.'

'It's the simple truth.' Max laughed, squeezed her hand, then went round the car to help her out. 'I'll see you safely inside, then get back to my retreat.'

* * *

The hotel bed was comfortable, but Abby lay awake for some time, her mind full of the eventful day which had begun with the surprisingly painful parting from her sister. Still at the mercy of her hormones, Laura had been a little tearful as she begged Abby to return soon and stay a lot longer. By that time, Domenico assured her, they would have moved into the new apartment with more rooms and a proper bed for Abby. After sharing a sofa with her little niece most of the night, Abby was glad to hear it. Isabella had needed much cuddling and reassurance to calm fears that Papa and Mamma wouldn't love her so much now they had a new boy baby. Abby had relayed the news to Isabella's shocked parents first thing next morning, and offered to look after baby Marco while they took their daughter out later for some kind of special treat.

'You're sure you're up for this?' Laura had asked before they left.

'Of course I am. If he yells, Auntie will sing to him. That should shut him up. *Ciao*, Bella.'

Isabella held her face up, mouth puckered for a kiss. '*Ciao*, Zietta.'

Domenico grinned. '*Ciao*, Auntie. Do I get a kiss too?'

'On the cheek,' warned Laura.

'Both cheeks,' said her handsome husband, suiting action to words before turning to kiss his wife full on her smiling mouth.

'For heaven's sake, go while Marco's quiet,' hissed Abby, laughing. 'You can do that sort of thing later.'

Abby smiled into the darkness. After providing a shoulder for more than one friend to cry on when a relationship went wrong, it was reassuring to know that everything was so obviously right with Laura's marriage. Which was more than could be said for Max Wingate's relationship with his mother. But it could hardly be sibling jealousy in his case, because he was obviously very fond of Gianni. Maybe he just didn't like his mother, though blessed with Isabel Green as a parent this was hard for Abby to imagine. But perhaps Max had never forgiven his mother for marrying again—which probably had a lot to do with the hardness in his eyes… Abby tried to shut him from her mind. She needed her beauty sleep if she wanted to look good when Max arrived to collect her.

Abby got up early next morning to pack before her breakfast arrived. Just before ten she went down to the foyer to find Max waiting for her, elegant in linen trousers and a formal shirt with a tie tucked in the pocket.

'Good morning,' he said, smiling. 'Did you sleep well?'

'Very well—after two nights on a sofa it was a treat to sleep in a bed. I just need to pay my bill.'

'No rush, I'm early. I'll take your gear out to the car.'

When Abby went out to join him, Max was leaning against the Range Rover looking into the distance, the sun gleaming on his sleek dark hair. On impulse she slipped her phone from her bag and took a surreptitious photograph of him. A souvenir of her trip to Todi, she told herself, then put the phone away quickly as he turned to smile at her.

'You're more relaxed today,' he commented later, as the car ate up the kilometres on the road to Perugia.

'Not so much in the way of hairpin bends on this route,' she pointed out. 'Besides, we met in stressful circumstances yesterday.'

'True.' He grinned. 'Right, then, Miss Green, fill me in on some background. You've heard a lot about my mother; tell me more about yours.'

Abby smiled affectionately. 'She's in her early fifties, but looks ten years younger. She's head teacher at the local primary school, blonde like my sister Laura, and a very attractive lady.'

'But she's never presented you with a stepfather. Would you have minded if she had?'

Abby thought about it. 'I don't honestly know. The three

of us were a pretty tight unit for years, and the cottage is small. Adding a stepfather to the mix could have caused problems, I suppose. But as far as I know the question never arose. Did you resent your stepfather?' she added.

He shook his head. 'I never thought of Enzo in that way because I lived with my own father in London. I just stayed at the Villa Falcone for the obligatory holiday every summer.'

'Is that the most your father would allow?'

'It was the most I would agree to at first.'

'You didn't like it there?'

'It wasn't the house. My feelings towards my mother were the problem.' He paused, his eyes on the road, then glanced at her briefly and went on. 'Luisa took a trip home alone to Todi just after my tenth birthday, met up with Enzo, childhood sweetheart transformed into wealthy businessman, and never came back.'

'And you never forgave her?'

His mouth tightened. 'I turned against her completely. I kicked up a terrible fuss when I eventually saw her again, because by then she had a new husband *and* a new baby.'

Abby kept quiet for a while, but curiosity eventually got the better of her. 'If you don't get on with your mother why did you build your retreat in Italy?'

'I didn't build it, exactly. I just designed the plans to put it back together. It had once been the home of Enzo Falcone's great-grandparents, and during those long summer holidays he used to take us up there for picnics. I loved the place so much he made me a present of the property when I was eighteen.' Max smiled crookedly. 'He liked me. Against all odds I liked him, too. And, stranger still, so did my father. Whenever Enzo came on business to London, as he did quite frequently, he'd take us both out to dinner. And because I was studying architecture Enzo trusted me to transform his old ruin into something beautiful one day.'

'You certainly did that. It's a magical place.'

'I'm glad you see it that way. Aldo the builder was all for knocking it down and starting from scratch, but to retain its character I wanted to incorporate as much of the original building as possible into my plans.'

'Was your stepfather pleased with the result?'

'Unfortunately, he died before it was finished. I miss him.' Max's face shadowed for an instant. 'Next time you come I'll show you the rest of it. I've converted the old threshing ground into a long, narrow pool, and the covered terrace outside the master bedroom looks out on the best view in the house.'

'Which is saying something,' said Abby, liking the sound of 'next time'.

Visited by a sudden, vivid picture of Abigail Green in the master bedroom, sharing it with him, Max slanted a glance at her. 'How did your sister come to marry an Italian?'

'Laura went to Venice on holiday. Domenico was asked to meet her at the airport and they are now living happily ever after.'

'Will that last?'

Abby nodded firmly. 'In spite of gloomy statistics, I'm certain it will.'

'Would you like something similar yourself?'

'Maybe. One day.'

'So there's no man in your life right now?'

'No.' Abby shrugged. 'Relationships tend to fall by the wayside because of my job. The most recent came to an end partly because the man wanted a woman he could see on Saturday nights without the drag of sitting through an easy-listening type of concert beforehand. Silas thought there was no other god but Mozart.'

Fool, thought Max with scorn. 'My tastes are a shade wider than that. I never tire of listening to Gianni, but I own up to a taste for the odd spot of jazz—even a burst of heavy metal on wilder days.'

'Do you have those often?'

He shot a glance at her. 'You'd be surprised.'

She laughed. 'I pictured you as another Mozart man.'

'Only when Gianni's performing it.'

They reached the colonnaded portico of Fontivegge station with an hour to spare before the train was due. Max went inside with Abby to confirm the change en route to Pisa, punched the ticket Domenico had bought for her into one of the yellow machines near the entrance to validate it, and then took her to the café to eat ham paninis with their espressos.

'Right,' said Max briskly, when it was time to make a move. 'At this point we exchange phone numbers, addresses, and any other pertinent information, Abigail Green.' He entered her number into his phone, then waited while she did the same with his, handed her a card with his address and home number, scrawled hers on the back of another and tucked it into his wallet.

'You've been such an enormous help,' said Abby, smiling at him gratefully. 'I've run out of ways to thank you.'

Max could think of several that would suit him down to the ground. 'Here's one. I'll be back in the UK at the weekend, so have lunch with me on Sunday. Say yes. Your train leaves soon.'

'Then, yes. I'd like that very much. Thank you—' She broke off with a laugh. 'There I go again!'

He smiled. 'Thank me again by reporting in tonight.'

'I will,' she promised, and looked at her watch. 'I'd better be on my way.'

'And I'd better get into my jacket and put this blasted tie on, ready to meet with my lady mother's approval.'

Max hefted her bag, his tall, lean body looking good to Abby in the kind of suit Italian tailors cut to such perfection. He took her hand in his as they walked along the concourse, and she liked the touch of it on her skin. She'd liked it the night before on their stroll round Todi, and suddenly wished quite violently that she wasn't about to say goodbye to Max Wingate. When her train was ready to board he reminded her to change in Florence, then took her in his arms.

'This is another way you can thank me.' He kissed her very thoroughly, holding her so tightly she was hot and breathless when he let her go. *'Arrivederci,'* he said huskily, and trailed a finger down her flushed cheek. 'Safe journey, Abby. Talk to me tonight.'

CHAPTER THREE

ABBY had armed herself with two paperbacks for the journey, but Max Wingate's kisses put paid to her concentration. She gazed at his photograph on her phone for a while, then pulled herself together and tried to read until the change in Florence. But the hard masculine face superimposed itself on the page, refusing to go away, and in the end she gave up and just stared through the train window as she went back over every detail of the magical evening in Todi.

On the flight from Pisa she ate some of the meal she was served to save bothering with supper when she got home, and at Heathrow took the taxi Simon would pay for. Once she arrived back in Bayswater, her basement flat seemed very quiet without Sadie. Abby missed her friend badly, not least her share of the rent. She sighed as she dumped her bags down. She had to find another job soon, or move to a cheaper flat.

Abby filled the kettle to make tea, then rang her mother to give her all the news about Marco Guido Chiesa, the most beautiful baby boy in the known world, and Isabella Anna Chiesa, his equally ravishing sister. Afterwards, as an exercise in self-control, she drank the entire mug of tea before allowing herself to ring Max.

'Hi. It's Abby. I'm back.'

'You're late. I've been waiting. Any problems on the way?'

'Other than tedium, none at all. How was your mother?'

'Startled to see me instead of Gianni, but we managed the entire trip from Perugia without crossing swords. Are you impressed?'

'Immensely. Was Gianni grateful?'

'Oh, yes. Luisa went all dewy-eyed when he embraced me so fervently. He begged me to stay on for a meal, so to please Rosa as much as anyone I did.'

'Will you see more of your mother while she's with Gianni?'

'No. I told her I had to get back to London.' He chuckled. 'She's very interested in you, by the way.'

'Me?'

'Gianni went on at great length about the beautiful young English lady who'd travelled all the way to Todi to finalise arrangements for his London concert. Luisa obviously considers such personal attention his rightful due, so I didn't spoil it by mentioning that the visit was just a detour from your trip to Venice.'

She laughed. 'So all went well at the family reunion?'

'Better than usual, certainly. I haven't seen Luisa for a while, so I suppose the session had novelty value.'

'Doesn't she mind seeing so little of you?'

'If she does she never says so,' he said, so brusquely Abby changed the subject.

'Did you find out anything about Gianni's mystery lady?'

'Not a damn thing. I wish to God I had. If she's someone's wife there'll be all kinds of hell to pay.'

'Do you think that's likely?'

'On one hand I doubt it. Gianni's a good Catholic boy, remember, also very wary of bad publicity. But he's also young, Italian, and madly in love. So who knows?'

'Do you think he'll tell you eventually?'

'Not with my mother around. Besides, I'm leaving shortly.

I have this important appointment to keep next Sunday, remember. I'll come for you at twelve.' He paused. 'It's going to be a long week until then, Abby. Goodnight, sleep well.'

The moment she disconnected, her phone rang again.

'Abby, at *last*! You've been engaged for ages. I know it's late but your mother said you were back tonight, and I couldn't wait.'

'Rachel? You sound a bit wired. Is something wrong?'

'No. Something's beautifully, wonderfully right! I'm engaged—third time lucky, and this time it really is the real thing.'

Abby's heart sank. Rachel Kent had been her friend since nursery school in Stavely, but she was also the one who most often needed Abby's shoulder to cry on when the latest 'real thing' went wrong. 'Tell me all about it, then. Who is he this time?'

Rachel gave a bubbling little laugh. 'It's Sam.'

Abby frowned. 'Sam who?'

'Sam Talbot, of course—now, be nice. Don't laugh, Abby.'

'I'm not laughing, just surprised.' Rachel had been engaged to Sam first time round. 'So when did this happen?'

'Today. The proposal, I mean. We met again at that wedding last month and I've been seeing him quite a lot since, but I didn't tell you—or anyone else—in case nothing came of it.' Rachel heaved an ecstatic sigh. 'Sam kept my ring all this time, Abby, isn't that romantic?'

'Absolutely. Mind you hang on to it this time.'

'I certainly will! Look, Abby, we're having a family lunch party at home to celebrate next Sunday, which is why I had to catch you the minute you got back. I know you're busy this time of year, but we arranged it especially for Sunday so you could be there.'

Abby winced. 'Rachel, I'm so sorry. I can't. I'm already booked that day.'

'Oh, *Abby*! Anyway, no problem. Bring this Silas of yours with you. Promise you'll come. You didn't make it to the other engagement parties, and this one is really important. Please, please say yes, Abby.'

'Oh, all right, Rachel, I'll be there,' said Abby, resigned. 'But no Silas. He's history.'

'Really? When did that happen?'

'When Sadie left to live with Tom. Silas took it for granted he could move in with me instead. I turned him down flat and he got quite nasty.'

'He didn't hit you or anything?' demanded Rachel fiercely.

'No. He just tried to rush me off to bed to show what I'd be missing.'

'Pig! You threw him out?'

'After a ludicrous little scuffle, yes. He keeps ringing me to grovel, and he's called round twice since, but I told him to get lost.'

'Good for you. Anyway, forget about Silas, love. I'll line up someone exciting for you instead.'

Rachel brushed away Abby's urgent protests, eager to know all about the new baby and the trip to Italy, until Abby stemmed the flow at last by congratulating her friend again before she rang off.

Abby looked at the kitchen clock, wondering if she should ring Max now. No. Better to leave it until tomorrow. Right now her disappointment was so intense she might even get tearful if she tried to tell him Sunday lunch was cancelled. And she didn't want him to know *quite* how much she'd been looking forward to seeing him again.

Next day was hectic as Abby caught up on correspondence and lent a hand with the summer brochures for the following year. Simon Hadley was delighted with the success of Abby's trip to the Villa Falcone, and asked, not for the first time, if she'd changed her mind about deserting him. Since she already had someone lined up for her job, Abby just laughed, and soon became knee-deep in arrangements for the concert on the following Saturday. It was so late by the time she got home she rang her mother the moment she was through the door.

'You must be shattered, darling,' said Isabel.

'It was hard going today,' admitted Abby. 'Anyway, are you all set for your trip tomorrow? Be warned, that sofa of Domenico's isn't too comfortable.'

'He wanted me to use his private apartment at the Forli Palace Hotel. His parents did that, but I don't fancy it on my own. I'm not going to be there long so I suggested sharing Isabella's room if he could put up some kind of folding bed in it.'

'Brilliant idea. She'll love that.'

'By the way, I heard all about Bella's special outing to Florian's with Mamma and Papa. Well done, Auntie—did Marco behave for you?'

'He was rather rowdy at one stage,' Abby admitted, laughing. 'But after I changed his nappy—I hope you're impressed—I walked him around for a bit, and he settled down in the end. My rendition of "Mull of Kintyre" put him out cold.'

Isabel chuckled. 'Thanks for the tip. You sound tired, darling, so have an early night. I'll ring when I get there, of course. And come down for a weekend the minute you leave your job. I've hardly seen anything of you for months.'

Abby promised, wished her mother *bon voyage*, and ate her supper before making the call to Max. To her intense frustration his mobile number was unobtainable and the only response from his house was a recorded message in two languages. He was probably playing chess with Aldo the builder, or happy families with Gianni and his mother. Or whoever. Max Wingate's social life was none of her business.

Next day was equally hectic, with overtime necessary to make up for a couple of hours off in the afternoon for a job interview. Abby got home late again, to find a message from Isabel, reporting safe arrival. After a long, hot bath Abby felt too weary to bother to dress again, and got into the camisole and briefs she slept in. She poached an egg for her supper and curled up on the sofa in her dressing gown to watch television, tired and yawning, but still too restless to go to bed. It was surprisingly hard to come back to earth after the Italian adventure. When the doorbell rang she leapt up irritably, in no mood for visitors. If it was Silas Wood he could just go away again. She snatched up the entry phone receiver to tell him that, and almost dropped it when she heard Max Wingate's voice.

'Abby? I should have rung first, but I took a chance on finding you in.'

'Max? What on earth are you doing here?' she said blankly.

'Standing outside the street door. Are you alone?'

'Yes, but—'

'Let me in, then. I've come a long way to see you.'

Casting a despairing look at her outfit, Abby pressed the release button, and fled to her bedroom to use a lipstick before she opened the door to a very different Max from the one who'd kissed her goodbye in Perugia. He seemed bigger than she remembered, his sleek hair was tousled, he needed a shave, and he looked altogether tougher and more formidable in jeans, boots and a leather jacket. In the face of such overpowering testosterone, Abby stared at him speechlessly.

Max smiled down into her startled eyes, fighting the urge to sweep her into his arms and kiss her senseless. 'Hello, Abby. Sorry it's so late.'

'Hi,' she responded huskily. 'This is a surprise.'

'Did I get you out of bed?'

'No.' Her mind raced over the contents of the fridge and her cupboards. 'Can I get you a glass of wine?'

'Dry white?' he asked, smiling.

'What else? I usually have a glass while I'm making supper, but I had a very busy day and I was so tired tonight I thought it might knock me flat…' Stop gabbling, she told herself, and took a mental inventory of her food supplies. 'I could throw some supper together for you.'

'No, thanks, I've eaten. And I'm driving so I'll pass on the wine.' Max looked down at her, an indulgent smile at the corners of his mouth. 'Relax. You're like a cat on hot bricks.'

'Of course I'm not,' she said brightly. 'Take off your jacket. I'll make coffee.'

The living room in the basement flat had always seemed perfectly adequate for two tall females to share, but it seemed crowded with the addition of Max Wingate. Abby filled the kettle and put out mugs, very conscious that he was watching her every move. She took biscuits from a tin and put them on a plate, her mind working overtime. It was late and he was a long way from Gloucestershire. Was he expecting to stay the night? Delighted though she was to see him, she wasn't up for that. She put the dish on the end of the low table nearest the scuffed leather club chair, handed Max his coffee and curled up on the sofa with her own.

'Thank you. I'm on my way to Kew to stay with my father for a night or two, but I thought I'd make a surprise visit here first.' He smiled crookedly. 'Not such a good idea from your point of view?'

So he had no intention of staying the night. Abby gave him a radiant smile. 'Actually it's a brilliant idea, because I need to talk to you urgently. I tried ringing you, but no luck.'

'What's wrong?'

'I can't make Sunday lunch after all.'

He masked a fierce stab of disappointment with a wry smile. 'Ah. You've got a better offer?'

She shook her head ruefully and told him about Rachel's engagement party. 'She's arranged it specifically for Sunday because I can't manage any other day at this time of year. So I have to go.'

Max's slanting eyebrows rose. 'If the lady is an old friend surely you want to go?'

'Of course.' Abby shrugged. 'But we haven't caught up with each other for a while, so she thought I'd be bringing Silas with me. The Mozart fan,' she added.

'Is the party here in London?'

'No, at Rachel's home in Stavely. I didn't make it to her other engagement parties, so I really must turn up at this one.'

He looked amused. 'How many has she had?'

'This is the third—well, sort of.' Abby grinned. 'Sam, the latest contender, is the one she was engaged to first time round.'

Max shook his head in mock respect. 'And he's willing to risk it a second time? Brave man.'

'Actually he's perfect for Rachel. She should have hung on to him in the first place. You'd like him.'

'Then take me to meet him—or was the invitation only for the Mozart-lover?'

Abby looked at him with dawning hope. 'You're willing to go to the party with me?'

He was willing to do anything in the world to make her happy, he realised, startled. 'Why not? I could drive you down, and we'd still achieve lunch together.'

'I'd like that.' She pulled a face. 'I admit I'd rather not go alone. If my mother had been home she would have gone with me, but—'

'But she's in Venice. So I'll go with you as protection.'

'From what?'

Max eyed her levelly. 'I don't know. You tell me.'

Abby hunched a shoulder. 'It's just that Rachel's such a matchmaker. She always insists on inviting some man she swears is perfect for me—and the result is disaster every time.'

Max ate a biscuit, frowning. 'Enlighten me. Why does

your friend feel obliged to hunt up men for someone as attractive as you?'

Thanking him for the compliment, Abby explained that, although she and Rachel were close, they were very different personalities. 'She can't function without a male presence in her life. I can and do, perfectly happily, but Rachel just can't accept a concept so alien to her. She keeps trying to pair me up with someone. '

'Is that why you steered clear of the other engagement celebrations?'

'No. I was in the middle of exams for the first one and in Venice the last time.' Abby smiled ruefully. 'Don't get me wrong—I love Rachel to bits, but her matchmaking drives me crazy.'

'Solution,' said Max, seizing the opportunity with relish. 'On Sunday, tell her I'm the replacement for the Mozart man.'

Abby eyed him dubiously. 'You won't laugh when she demands your intentions.'

'As you virtually did when I turned up just now?' He wagged an admonishing finger. 'You thought I'd come for a sleepover, Abigail Green.'

'Of course I didn't,' she lied. 'I was just surprised to see you. Why did you cut your holiday short?'

Max settled comfortably in the chair, his long legs outstretched. 'Two reasons. One, I saw no point in waiting until Sunday to see you again. Two, I'm a coward.'

She eyed him in scorn. 'Oh, come on! I haven't known you long, but the last bit's hard to swallow.'

'Thank you kindly.' Max's mouth turned down. 'However, I've had Gianni begging me not to say a word about his *innamorata*, and Luisa firing questions at me because she harbours suspicions about his love-life. I insisted, with almost perfect truth, that I knew nothing about it, so she eventually gave up. But she won't rest until she finds out from some other source. I'd never thought of myself as a coward before, but to make sure I'm elsewhere when the balloon goes up I altered the train reservation for my car and got out of the way.'

Abby chuckled. 'Leaving Gianni all alone and defenceless.'

'Anything but! Rosa's the perfect bodyguard. Luisa knows better than to try to winkle it out of *her*.'

'You really think the love of his life is married, then?'

'Gianni's so desperate to keep her identity secret I'm beginning to think she must be—or at least spoken for.' Max grimaced. 'I suppose I should have stayed to pick up the pieces, but where Luisa's concerned my presence usually makes things worse.'

'Maybe she still feels guilty.'

His eyebrows shot together. 'Guilty?'

'For deserting you all those years ago.'

He gave a cynical laugh. 'I doubt that.'

'She's a Catholic?'

'Yes.'

'And she deserted her son and her husband and married someone else. Of course she feels guilty. If not all the time, certainly every time she sees you, Max—' She stopped, flushing a little. 'Sorry. It's none of my business.'

He shook his head. 'I've made it your business. I've never confided so much in a woman in my entire life.'

A statement which pleased Abby enormously. 'You must have known a few in your time, surely!'

'Of course. In fact,' added Max casually, 'some of the relationships lasted quite a while. The last fell by the wayside because I was too wrapped up in work to pay the necessary attention to it.' He looked round at the small room. 'Has anyone shared this place with you, Abby?'

She nodded. 'Sadie Morris, who was up at Trinity College with me, but she moved in with her boyfriend a couple of weeks ago. I'm keeping it up on my own until I know what I'm doing next.'

Max gave a sudden yawn and, apologising, took out his phone. 'I'd better ring Dad and say I'm on my way.' He got to his feet. 'What time do you get home in the evening?'

'Whenever I finish for the day—usually fairly late.'

'Have you anything planned for tomorrow night?'

'No.'

'Will you be home by eight?'

'I could be,' she said with caution.

'Then I'll be here at eight-fifteen to take you out some-where. What do you say?' he added, smiling at her.

Abby didn't hesitate. 'I say, yes please. Only I'll probably be too tired to go out. Would you mind eating here instead?'

'Not if that's what you prefer,' he assured her. 'Tell me which type of cuisine you like and I'll bring dinner with me.'

'No need. I'll visit my favourite deli in my lunch-hour.'

'Not a chance. You're working. If that's your choice I'll find a deli myself somewhere.' Max put a finger under her chin. 'Go to bed and get some sleep.'

'Yes, sir!'

He grinned and kissed her briefly, then released her to pick up his jacket. 'Goodnight, Abby. Sweet dreams.'

In her bedroom later, Abby chuckled as she looked in the mirror. No make-up, hair left to its own devices to dry, and a towelling dressing gown long past its prime. And she'd been worried that Max intended to stay the night! It was a wonder he'd even stayed for coffee. But he wanted to see her again tomorrow, she thought with satisfaction, so maybe it was the beauty of her mind that attracted him.

Abby spent next day in a hectic round of checking up on hotel bookings and the dressing rooms at the concert venue, but when she got back to base she told Simon she needed to get home a bit earlier for once.

'Hot date?' he asked indulgently. 'Dash off, then. Have fun.'

Abby smiled to herself as she travelled home. The kind of evening she was looking forward to would probably sound nothing like fun to friends who led a more hectic social life than hers. She'd enjoyed the parties and rowdy pub evenings of her student days with a crowd of both sexes, including the summer balls. Since living in London she'd been out now and again with men she'd met in the course of her job, but she enjoyed evenings out with girlfriends just as much, sometimes more. With Max Wingate it was the prospect of a peaceful night *in* that sent her running along the street of tall old houses in Bayswater. She unlocked the outer door in the pillared portico and raced down the stairs to her flat, fumbling with her key in her eagerness to get in.

She shed her clothes in a tearing hurry to get in the shower, laughing at herself as she turned on the spray. Rachel went wild with excitement in these situations, not Abigail Green. But for once Abby knew how she felt. And it felt good. By eight she was ready, in slouchy gold velvet trousers and a thin black sweater, humming as she did a last-minute tidy-up in the flat. She grabbed the receiver when the doorbell rang at exactly eight-fifteen, breathless as she answered it.

'I'm here,' said Max.

'Come down, then.' She pressed the button for the outer door, opened her own and left it ajar. A minute later Max gave a perfunctory knock and strode in laden with packages. Without a word he dumped them on the floor, took her in his arms and kissed her until her head reeled.

'I needed that,' he said simply, and grinned into her dazed eyes as he closed the door behind him. 'Hi.'

'Hi,' she said breathlessly. It wasn't just her mind, then. 'You're punctual.'

'I had incentive.' The intent eyes gave her a long, thorough scrutiny from head to toe. *'Delizioso*, Miss Green.'

'Why, thank you, Mr Wingate,' she said demurely. 'What have you brought? I'm hungry.'

'Good, so am I,' he said in approval, and picked up the bags. 'I don't know your preferences—yet—so I'll unpack this lot and you can choose.'

They were soon settled opposite each other at the table, with a basket of bread and a platter of cheese in front of them as they made inroads on plates heaped with the delicacies that had caught Max's fancy.

'It would probably have been cheaper for you to take me out,' said Abby. 'But after a long day of nose to the grindstone I much prefer this.'

He grinned as he refilled their wine glasses. 'And this way you get leftovers and we're free of amorous waiters.'

'The one in Todi was very sweet,' protested Abby.

'He was a pest!'

'How was your father?' she asked hastily.

'Fit as a fiddle. He asked the usual questions about my mother and Gianni, and this time I had more to say because I'd actually seen Luisa.'

Abby eyed him with sympathy. 'It must be an awkward situation for you.'

'Actually, it isn't.' Max pushed the platter of cheese towards her. 'Dad always asks about Luisa, but I think he's a lot more interested in Gianni these days. Dad's a keen music lover, and follows my little brother's career very closely. He was tickled pink about my escape from the fallout over the secret lover.'

Abby helped herself to a wedge of deliquescent Brie. 'How are things at the Villa Falcone?'

'Peaceful as of early this evening. I rang Gianni before I came from Kew tonight. He's rehearsing like mad to keep out of his mother's way.' Max grinned. 'She's been plaguing Rosa, apparently, but she might as well save her breath.'

'Does Rosa have children of her own?'

'No. Luisa had such a bad time when Gianni was born, Enzo engaged Rosa to look after the baby from day one. To Rosa he's the son she never had, so Luisa won't get her to say a thing.' He shrugged. 'I told him to put his *mamma* on a train to Venice, say goodbye to the love of his life and take off for Rome a couple of days early to concentrate on his performance.'

'Will he do that?'

'Yes, because the concert will be televised live, so it means a lot to him. The camera loves Gianni because he doesn't pull faces when he sings. Besides, if it's to further his career Luisa will do anything he asks.' Max smiled at her. 'And that is quite enough about my relatives. Tell me what you've been doing today.'

'Dashing about all over the place to check on the arrangements for Saturday. It's my farewell concert, so I'm making doubly sure everything goes smoothly.' Abby sat back and pushed her plate away, smiling at him. 'That was perfect. Just what I needed. My cue to say thank you again.'

'I'll do the clearing up. Don't worry,' he added, 'I'll put all the leftovers in the right containers and stow them in your fridge. I live alone, remember, I'm used to this kind of thing.'

'But I bet you own a dishwasher—and you probably have a cleaner in your place in Pennington, too.'

'Two of life's essentials,' he agreed as he collected plates.

Abby carried the remains of the cheese and bread to the counter. 'I can't just sit and watch, Max.'

'In that case make the coffee I brought.'

Because it was impossible to keep out of each other's way in the sliver of kitchen, there was a lot of jostling and laughter before Max finally carried the coffee tray to the low table in front of the sofa.

'So when are you going back to Pennington?' asked Abby, securing a lock of hair behind one ear.

Max sat back, taking great pleasure in watching her teeth catch in her cushiony bottom lip as she poured the coffee. 'I'll drive down tomorrow and look in at the office, but I'm not officially due back until next week, so I'll drive up to Kew again on Friday. Let's do this again in the evening. I'll take you out this time.'

'Oh, Max, I'm sorry. I can't on Friday,' she said with regret. 'Simon's organised a leaving party for me.'

'Damn. I'll have to possess my soul in patience until Sunday, then.' Max put his cup down and turned towards her. 'In that case give me a briefing now. Should I buy the happy pair a present?'

'No. Rachel was adamant about that. She's had to return two batches of gifts already, so I'll save up for a wedding present instead.' She apologised as a sudden yawn engulfed her.

'You're tired, Abby.' He frowned. 'You're likely to be even more tired by Sunday morning, but you can sleep in the car on the way down.'

'I wouldn't dream of wasting time with you in sleep.' She flushed, her eyes daring him to take it as a *double entendre*.

Manfully ignoring the visions that filled his mind, Max eyed her questioningly. 'What happens next in your life? Do you have something lined up?'

She nodded. 'I've had a couple of interviews already, including one yesterday with some hedge-fund managers who need a presentable, non-smoking PA capable of dealing with corporate entertaining.'

'Did they grab you with both hands?'

'They had other people to see, but to be honest I'm not keen.' She shrugged. 'For some time now I've been seriously considering a job nearer home, so I can see more of my mother.' Abby looked him in the eye. 'Long before I met you,

Mr Wingate, I made the decision to give up city life and look for work in Pennington.'

He took her hand in his, his fingers smoothing it as he smiled into her eyes. 'From my point of view it's the ideal arrangement. And there must be plenty of openings for personable non-smoking graduates of your experience—particularly one who went to school there.'

'I hope you're right. I might earn less by way of salary, but flat rental would be cheaper than London.'

'And you could see more of me as well as your mother,' he pointed out.

Abby smiled demurely. 'An added bonus, of course.'

His hand tightened on hers. 'Do you believe in fate, Abby?'

'If you mean do I believe that some things happen to us beyond our control, yes, I do.' She grinned at him. 'But I also believe in giving fate a helping hand.'

He laughed and raised her hand to his lips. 'A girl after my own heart.'

She shook her head in mock reproof. 'I think of myself as a woman, Mr Wingate!'

'So do I, far too much, which brings me straight to the point.' His eyes held hers. 'Fate brought us together in Umbria, Abigail Green. But what happens from now on is entirely up to us.'

CHAPTER FOUR

Abby looked at him in silence for an interval, her pulse racing. 'What,' she said at last, 'do you mean, exactly?'

Max smoothed a finger over the back of her hand. 'First, I should explain that you're something new in my life.'

'Could you be more specific?'

He smiled wryly. 'I suppose you could say that my feelings for you are the kind normally reserved only for Gianni.'

Her eyebrows rose. *'Brotherly?'*

He winced. 'Hell, no! I meant protective, not fraternal. Laugh if you like, but almost from the start I've felt this urge to take care of you.'

'I'm not laughing,' she said slowly. 'Up to now the only man I've met who feels like that towards me is Domenico.'

'You like your sister's husband a lot, obviously.'

'I would try to like anyone who made Laura so happy, but with Domenico I don't have to try.' Abby looked at him curiously. 'This protective feeling of yours—is that why you drove me to Perugia? Just to make life easier for me?'

'It was part of it. But I also wanted to spend every possible minute with you until you left. And,' he added wryly, 'wipe out your first impression of me.'

She chuckled. 'You did that just by wining and dining me in Todi—over and above the call of duty.'

'No duty. It was pure pleasure—except that I had to deliver you to your hotel without even kissing you goodnight.' He raised an eyebrow. 'Could you tell how much I objected to that?'

She shook her head. 'You hide your feelings very well.'

He grinned. 'Unlike you, Abby. When I turned up here out of the blue last night you were pole-axed. Come clean. You thought my goodbye kiss in Perugia meant I'd come to hustle you straight to bed.'

She smiled sheepishly. 'You can hardly blame me. Some expect that in return for just the outlay on dinner, whereas you'd come all the way from Italy.'

'Yet you opted to stay in with me tonight?'

'Yes. My gut instinct told me you wouldn't rush me to bed the minute I swallowed my supper,' she said bluntly.

'Your instinct was right.' He put a finger under her chin to turn her face up to his. 'Any rushing to bed, however hotly I fancy the idea, must be done by you. I admit it's not my usual *modus operandi* with a woman—'

'I object to your phrasing, Max Wingate,' she said severely.

'Don't tell me your Latin isn't up to it, Miss Swot!'

'I meant that I don't want to hear about other women.'

'Subject dropped,' he said promptly.

'So if we do see more of each other you'll do only what *I* want?' asked Abby, her pulse accelerating at the gleam in his eyes.

'I make no promises,' he warned. 'What do you have in mind?'

'Right now I just want you to kiss me,' she said simply.

His eyes blazed in disbelief for an instant, then he crushed her close and kissed her until they were both shaken and breathless.

'As is patently obvious,' he said gruffly, when he could speak, 'feeling protective doesn't rule out wanting to make love to you. You'd better take that on board from the start.'

Abby heaved in a deep, unsteady breath. 'Got it. But instead of sweeping me off my feet you expect me to sweep you off yours?'

'Absolutely—the sooner the better.'

'I'll keep that in mind.' She eyed him challengingly. 'But there's something you must take on board, too. Any relationship between us, however casual or brief, would have to be exclusive.'

'No worries there.' His eyes hardened. 'I take a dim view of infidelity.'

Of course he did. She grinned at him to lighten the mood. 'So, now that's settled, do we cut our wrists and mingle our blood?'

'Is that normal practice for you?' he said, laughing, and kissed her wrists instead.

'There is no normal practice,' Abby informed him, charmed by the gesture. 'I've been out with men from time to time since I've lived in London, of course, but there's been nothing you could glorify with the word relationship.'

'Amazing! Surely some of them must have wanted more?'

'Yes. But at that point I always said goodbye.'

His eyes darkened. 'Say that to me and I'll ignore you.'

Her eyes danced. 'Not much point in my saying it, then!'

'Exactly.' He kissed her again, then gently pushed her away. 'But it's time *I* said goodbye. It's getting late and you're working tomorrow. I should go.'

'No, please, not yet!'

'You want me to, I'll stay!' Max put his arms round her, smoothing his cheek over her hair. 'So what happens on Sunday? We turn up at your friend's house and you introduce me as what?'

Abby tipped her head back to grin at him. 'What do you fancy? Friend? Boyfriend?'

His eyes glinted. 'How about lover?'

'In Stavely? Please! Besides, you're not,' she pointed out.

'Not yet!' He sighed heavily. 'Nor right now, either, because you have to do the rushing off to bed part.'

'I'd forgotten that.'

'I wish I had,' said Max with feeling. He held her close in a secure, undemanding embrace Abby found so comfortable that her eyelids began to droop. At last he got up reluctantly and drew her to her feet. 'You're tired. I'll take off and let you get some sleep.' He smiled down at her. 'This was good tonight. I enjoyed it.'

'Me too. As you probably noticed, I didn't want it to end,' she pointed out sleepily. 'I'll see you on Sunday.'

'Try not to work too hard until then. What time does your concert finish on Saturday? After the fat lady sings?'

'No. After the firework display is over and everyone else has left.'

'How do you get home?'

'I organise a taxi beforehand.'

'Excellent.' He collected his jacket and took her hand to make for the door. 'I must find one myself right now. Goodnight, Abby.'

'Goodnight. Oh, and Max,' she added suddenly, then changed her mind. 'I forgot to say thank you again,' she improvised as he raised an eyebrow.

'My pleasure, in every way possible—almost.' He kissed her again and went out.

Abby stared blankly at the door he'd closed behind him. After practically begging him to stay longer she'd only just avoided asking Max to ring her tomorrow night as well. This was new. It had always been the men in her life who wanted to stay longer, and rang her up far too often. Sadie had constantly teased her about it. 'One day, Miss Cool, you'll fall just like the rest of us,' she'd prophesied.

* * *

Outside in the road, Max flagged down a taxi and sat back on the way to Kew, deep in thought. He'd enjoyed the evening far more than anything remotely similar in the past. Over the years he'd eaten a fair number of meals intended to present the cook as ideal wife material, but if the way to a man's heart was supposed to be via his stomach it had never worked for him. Yet tonight, over a few bits and pieces from a delicatessen, he'd found it only too easy to imagine sharing meals and everything else in his life—not least his bed—on a permanent basis with Abigail Green. It was hard to put a finger on what set her apart from the rest. Her looks were undeniable but they were subtle, the intelligence behind them a lot to do with the attraction. And there was a touch-me-not air about her that called to him so strongly it had taken every ounce of willpower he possessed to keep from carrying her off to bed. The sole thing holding him back had been the risk of ending things between them before they'd started.

Abby drifted on autopilot through preparations for bed, wondering dreamily what Sadie would say when she heard that her prophesy looked like coming true. Not that it had yet, exactly, but the 'Miss Cool' tag no longer applied. She felt a response to Max Wingate she'd never felt before, all the more powerful because he made it clear that he was happy, or at least willing to let her set the pace of their—their what? Relationship? Love affair? Neither seemed to fit. One thing was certain. She wanted the time to fly until she saw him again on Sunday morning.

Late on Saturday night, Abby felt sad when the music was over and the final burst of fireworks faded in the sky. As the crowds dispersed and the lights went out on the stage, she began to wonder if she'd made a huge mistake in giving it all up. But when the last goodbyes were said, and she was in the taxi on the way home, Abby felt a lift of spirits at the thought of seeing Max again in a few hours. Given the choice she would have preferred a quiet Sunday together rather than the drive down to Stavely for Rachel's party, but on the plus side she would be with him for most of the day. And there was a message from him on her phone when she got in.

'Go straight to bed, and sleep well. I'll see you in the morning.'

Abby smiled as she played the message, and went to sleep the moment her head hit the pillow.

When she let Max in next morning he took her in his arms and kissed her at length, then stood back, a look in his eyes which brought colour to her cheeks. 'Good morning, Abigail Green. I thought you'd be tired and wan after your farewell concert, but you're blooming.'

She smiled demurely. 'Probably because I slept well.'

'I think there's more to it than that! Will I do, by the way? I forgot to ask about dress code.'

Since his suit was the lightweight masterpiece he'd worn to meet his mother in Perugia, Abby nodded with enthusiasm. 'Great suit.'

'Great dress!'

'Concert clothes,' she said, smiling. Her clinging crêpe jersey dress showed off the length of leg she was rather vain about, and the colour matched her eyes almost exactly. But any glow was more to do with the prospect of a day spent in Max's company than clothes and cosmetics.

On the drive down Abby described the concert in detail, confessing that she'd suffered a few pangs at the thought of its being her last. 'I got the other job, by the way,' she added casually. 'I heard from the hedge managers on Friday.'

Max kept his eyes on the traffic. 'Congratulations.'

'But I've set my heart on a job in Pennington so I turned

it down.' She pulled a face. 'Which was a bit arrogant, without anything in view yet, but the job didn't really appeal to me. And Simon's been very generous. I won't starve while I go job-hunting.'

Max reached out a hand to touch hers. 'No, you won't.'

'I was joking!'

'I'm not. In any way.'

Things were moving too fast, thought Abby. It was scary. 'I'll be fine for a while,' she said brightly. 'I quite fancy the idea of a lull at home before getting back out there.'

He chuckled. 'I fancy the idea, too. Having you twenty miles or so away with your mother is a damn sight better than thinking of you in London, surrounded by randy hedge managers all day.'

'The ones I met at the interview were rather charming!'

'I bet they were.' He slanted a swift smile at her. 'Don't worry, Abby. I'm not rushing you into anything.'

'I know,' she said, resigned. 'It's up to me to do the rushing.'

He let out a crack of laughter. 'I can't wait—no,' he amended quickly, 'that's not true. For you, Abigail Green, I can, and will.'

When they arrived in Stavely Abby gave directions down Springfield Lane to show Max round Briar Cottage before going on to the party.

'Welcome to the family home,' she said, unlocking the front door, and Max stooped his head and followed her into the small, inviting parlour.

'Great house,' he commented, looking round.

'Small house, you mean,' she said, laughing. 'Come into the kitchen. Stretch your legs with a stroll round the garden, if you like, while I powder my nose.'

'Does your mother do all that herself?' asked Max when he came in. 'It's a lot of work for someone who holds down a job like hers.'

Abby went over to the window to look objectively at the garden. It stretched for quite a way behind the house, and for the first time it came home to her how much work it took to look after the lawn and surrounding shrubs and keep the high laurel hedges in trim. Directly outside the window there was a small patio edged with a beautifully tended rockery. More work.

'I do a bit when I'm down,' she said thoughtfully. 'But you're right. I never appreciated how much time Mother puts in out there.'

'Does she have someone to help her?'

Abby gave him a guilty look. 'I don't know—which is terrible, because I should know.' She dived into her bag as the ring tone jingled on her phone. 'It's a text from Rachel, telling me to hurry up,' she said, looking at it. 'Are you ready for this?'

Max took her in his arms and kissed her very thoroughly. 'Now I am,' he said at last, smiling down at her.

'And now I'm not,' she scolded. 'I need another tidy-up. And so do you. I've left my brand on you.'

'That you have,' he agreed, with a look that melted her bones.

The Kent home was a rambling Edwardian house with a big, rambling garden to match, plus a large bumpy paddock the Range Rover moved over with ease to park at the end of a line of cars. Max opened Abby's door and grinned as he saw her shoes. 'This grass is wet, and those are not meant for hiking around in fields.'

'I'd forgotten about the paddock,' said Abby, resigned, then gave a little squeak as he scooped her up and strolled over to the fence to set her down on the relatively dry surface of the drive on the other side. 'Thank you,' she said breathlessly, as he ducked under the fence to join her.

'Any excuse to hold you in my arms,' he assured her, and took her hand. 'Ready?'

As they approached the open front door of the house Rachel flew from it, with Sam in laughing pursuit. She flung her arms round Abby and kissed her, eyeing Max with avid curiosity.

'I'm Max Wingate,' he said, with a slight bow.

Sam held out his hand, panting, and introduced himself.

Max smiled. 'Congratulations to both of you. Abby said you wouldn't mind if I gatecrashed your party.'

'Of course we don't mind, we're delighted,' Rachel assured him as she shook his hand. She exchanged a sparkling blue look with Abby. 'She's kept very quiet about you, but any friend of Abby's is welcome in this house.'

'And will be in ours when our house-hunting is successful,' added Sam, and kissed Abby. 'Great to see you again.'

'You too, Sam,' she said, and patted his cheek. 'Congratulations—again. Hang on to her this time.'

'Tooth and nail,' he promised, and put an arm round Rachel. 'Come on, darling, let's get these people inside and give them a drink.'

Cicely Kent enveloped Abby in a warm hug then put her away to look at her. 'I'm so glad you could make it, dear. How gorgeous you look. Such a shame your mother is away. Before you go you must tell me all about Laura's new baby.'

'I will.' Abby kissed her affectionately. 'Lovely to see you. Let me introduce Max Wingate, the friend who drove me down.'

'How do you do, Mrs Kent,' Max said smoothly. 'I hope you don't mind an extra guest.'

'Of course not. Any friend of Abby's is welcome here.' She smiled at him in approval. 'She's just like a second daughter, though we see far too little of her lately.' She wagged an admonishing finger at Abby. 'But someone here will be rather disappointed that you've brought a friend—must dash and see to the caterers.' She beckoned to a waiter with a tray of drinks. 'Have fun. I'll see you later.'

'She means Marcus, Abby,' said Rachel. 'I couldn't find anyone exciting for you in time, but it doesn't matter, because you brought someone exciting with you!'

'Other guests are arriving, Rachel,' said a familiar voice. Abby turned to greet a tall, smiling man with sleek fair hair. 'You look ravishing, Abigail. How are you? Long time no see.'

She smiled serenely. 'Hi, Marcus. Let me introduce Max Wingate. He drove me down today. Max, this is Marcus Kent, Rachel's brother.'

'Glad to know you,' said Marcus, shaking hands. 'Are you London-based, like Abby?'

'Pennington these days.' Max took two glasses from the tray offered by a waiter. 'Here you are, darling.' He handed one to Abby and put a possessive arm round her as he touched his glass to hers. 'To the happy pair.'

Marcus echoed the toast. 'Let's hope Rachel sticks to Sam this time.'

'I'm sure she will,' said Abby firmly. 'Would you excuse us, Marcus? There are some people here I'd like Max to meet.'

She took Max away on a round of introductions to neighbours and friends, eager for news of Laura's new baby and an introduction to the man in Abigail Green's life, but when the lunch gong sounded Rachel and Sam beckoned them to one of the small tables set up on the terrace outside.

'Let's sit together to eat,' said Rachel. 'Abby and I don't see enough of each other these days.'

'You may soon,' said Abby. 'I'm looking for a job in Pennington.'

'Wonderful,' said Rachel, delighted.

Sam and Rachel looked so happy together, and Max was such an effortless guest, that Abby was glad that she'd made the effort to come. The lunch was a long, lazy affair, ending in numerous toasts and speeches, but when they were over at last Abby got up to kiss Rachel and Sam goodbye.

'Max has to drive me to London, and then back to Pennington afterwards, so it's time we were on our way.'

'Going so soon?' said Marcus, joining them. 'As usual, you're very sparing with your company, Miss Green.'

'We'll see a lot more of her in future. She's giving up her events job,' Rachel informed him.

'If you're in need of a change, Abby,' said Marcus swiftly, 'there'll be an opening in my chambers soon.'

She shook her head, conscious of Max stiffening beside her. 'Not my field, I'm afraid. And, unlike Dr Johnson, I've had enough of London for a while. I want something nearer home. But thanks for the thought.'

'Time we said goodbye to our hostess,' said Max, putting an arm round her again. He congratulated Rachel and Sam once more, said goodbye to Marcus Kent and took Abby across the room to Cicely Kent to be hugged and kissed, and to give promises to come again soon.

When they were on their way at last Abby asked to stop off at Briar Cottage for a breather. 'If we call in at the farm first I can get some milk. I need lots of tea before we head back to London.'

When they reached the farm, Max ordered Abby and her shoes to stay put. He crossed the yard to knock on the kitchen door and eventually returned with the strapping figure of the farmer she'd known all her life. Chris Morgan handed over a dozen eggs with the milk, smiling affectionately.

'You look a picture, Abby,' he said, leaning in at the car window. 'You've been celebrating with Rachel? Young Sam Talbot should superglue that ring to her finger.'

'I'll pass the suggestion on,' said Abby, chuckling. 'But I'm sure it's for keeps this time. How are things with you and yours, Chris?'

'Great, thanks. Jane will be sorry to have missed you. She's off with our tribe at a Young Farmers rally and I'm holding the fort.' He turned to Max. 'Good to meet you. Come again and have a look round the farm.'

Max agreed warmly. 'I'd like to. Great outfit you've got here. Damned hard work, though.'

Chris nodded. 'But my sons are shaping up to share it these days, thank God.'

When they were bumping their way back along the farm track, Max asked in a dry tone if there were any more childhood friends he should meet.

'Not right now.' Abby eyed him in surprise. 'Didn't you like Chris?'

'I did, very much. A few minutes' acquaintance told me that what you see is what you get with a man like that, the same with young Sam Talbot, too. Rachel's damn lucky to get a second chance.'

'She knows that. When we managed a few private moments together Rachel said they're getting married as soon as they can.' Abby yawned as they reached Briar Cottage. 'Sorry. How do you feel about an hour or so of doing nothing before we start back?'

'Enthusiastic. I hope you noticed that I worked my socks off to make a good impression today.'

'I did, and you succeeded.' She grinned at him as he helped her out. 'Rachel was very impressed.'

Max looked her in the eye. 'Unlike her brother—he disliked me on sight.'

Abby shrugged, and went up the path ahead of him to unlock the door. 'You imagined it.'

Max followed her into the kitchen, and put the eggs and milk on the table. 'He certainly doesn't dislike you.'

'He's known me for years—thinks of me as a kid sister, like Rachel.' She kicked off her shoes and filled the kettle, avoiding the dark, intent gaze.

'His reaction to you today was a long way from fraternal, Abby.'

'You're exaggerating,' she said flatly, pouring boiling water into mugs. She added a splash of milk and put them on the table, then sat down.

Max took off his jacket and sat opposite, but the easy camaraderie of earlier was missing. At last Abby put down her cup and looked him in the eye.

'So, what's wrong?'

'I soon realised why you needed protection today. It wasn't from some unknown hopeful Rachel was likely to dream up for you. It was from Marcus Kent.' The hard eyes held hers until Abby conceded defeat.

'Only to save me embarrassment,' she said defensively. 'I had a schoolgirl crush on Marcus when I was young. He knew it only too well, and never lets me forget it.'

'Do you still have it?'

'Lord, no. It died a natural death when I left school.'

'If anyone's got a crush these days it's Marcus Kent. On you.' Max held her eyes very deliberately. 'I object to that.'

She smiled. 'Is that why you called me darling and kept putting your arm round me?'

'Partly. But mainly because it seemed like the natural thing to do. So does this.'

He got up and pulled her out of her chair into his arms, the sudden savagery of his kiss taking her breath away. He drew her hard against him, his mouth devouring hers as fingers caressed her breasts through the clinging fabric. She felt her nipples harden as he pushed her dress aside, and shivered as his seeking fingers seared through the thin covering of lace underneath. Darts of fire streaked through her body in a delicious response she'd never experienced before, and after a long, heated interval she broke away to look up at him, breathing raggedly, her eyes glittering in her flushed face.

'Is this where I rush you to bed, Max?' she asked huskily, and saw the heavy lids drop to mask the hunger she could see so clearly in his eyes while her heart hammered against her ribs.

'Why now, Abby?' he demanded harshly.

'Because it seems like the natural thing to do,' she whispered, and held up her mouth for his kiss.

With a muffled groan Max took what she offered. With her slender, yielding body in his arms, it was hard to refuse her when every instinct was screaming at him to push her flat and bury himself deep inside her.

Suddenly she pulled away, holding out an impatient hand. 'Are you coming then?' she demanded.

Max drew in a deep breath. The need to make love to her was consuming him, roaring like fire in his veins, but some hard-won shred of control made him shake his head. 'No, Abby.'

She dropped his hand like a hot cake, her eyes wide in such mortified dismay Max cursed himself for being an over-principled fool.

'You don't want me after all?' she said, her voice catching.

'Of course I want you,' he said roughly. 'I want you so much I'm in physical pain right this minute. But you don't really want me, Abby. Or, if you do, not for the right reasons.'

She looked at him in silence for a moment. 'Exactly what kind of reasons do you require, then?' she demanded.

'The normal kind, when a man and woman desire each other so much they can't exist for another second without making love.' Max took her hand and looked down into her face. 'Can you honestly say you felt like that just now?'

Abby thought about lying, but something in the dark eyes demanded the truth. 'Not exactly, but I did want you to make love to me. Don't worry,' she choked suddenly, flinging away. 'I don't any more.'

Max's last shred of control deserted him. He spun her round, picked her up and strode into the other room to sit down on the sofa, holding her cruelly tight as he kissed her protesting mouth. He caught a flailing hand as he kissed her into submission, and felt a surge of triumph as her lips finally parted to receive his seeking tongue. He sat her upright, slid down the zip of her dress and pushed it from her shoulders down to her waist. He heard her shocked intake of breath as he thrust the thin barrier of lace aside to renew his attentions to her small, pointing breasts, taking fierce pleasure in her reaction when she writhed against him in helpless response to his lips and grazing teeth.

Driven by a basic need to conquer, Max bore her down beneath him, and Abby gasped, her entire body on fire as he caressed her. When his skilled, hungry mouth returned to hers, she yielded to him, rapidly learning the lesson he was teaching her as hot, damp response pooled deep down inside her. Suddenly she wanted him so badly she felt she'd scream if he didn't take her. They breathed in ragged unison as he kissed his way down her throat and breasts, and she thrust her hips against his erection, winning a deep, visceral groan in response. But when he slid a caressing, seeking hand up her thigh, she breathed in sharply, stiffening in familiar panic, and wrenched herself away.

'Stop, *please*. I can't do this. I'm sorry, sorry…' She sat up and turned her back on him, head bowed, and without a word Max got to his feet and strode from the room.

CHAPTER FIVE

ABBY put herself back together with clumsy, shaking fingers, then sat slumped on the edge of the sofa, wishing she had a magic carpet to whisk her away to her room in Bayswater. When the door opened she tensed, and turned her head away to avoid the inevitable scorn and distaste in Max Wingate's eyes.

He walked across the room and stood so close she could feel the heat of his body. 'Look at me,' he ordered.

She shook her head violently, but he put a finger under her chin and turned her face up to his, his eyes locked on hers. 'A woman always has the right to say no, Abby.'

She heaved in a deep, unsteady breath, relaxing slightly when she saw he wasn't furious. 'Thank you. Not every man agrees with you on that. But normally in these situations the U-turn comes sooner. Much sooner.'

Max felt something hard and cold inside him dissolve. 'This happens often?'

She nodded miserably. 'I wouldn't say often. And never like this before.'

He took her by the hand. 'Let's make more tea.'

'The panacea for all ills,' said Abby numbly, and let him take her into the kitchen.

Good, thought Max. At least she didn't shy away.

'I'm sorry,' she said contritely. 'I'm not really a teaser.'

'I know,' he said, with such tenderness her eyes filled.

'I'm not usually a watering pot, either.'

'God, I hope not. I can't handle it when women cry.'

Abby recovered enough to give him a friendly punch on the arm as they went into the kitchen. 'Do the women you know cry a lot, then?'

Max pulled a face. 'One or two in the past.'

'Not my style.' Abby gave him a crooked little smile. 'I've got a confession to make.'

Max braced himself. 'What is it?'

'I'm hungry!'

He felt a wave of such relief wash through him, he sat down at the kitchen table instead of pulling her into his arms as he so badly wanted to. 'No surprise there—you ate very little at the party.'

She turned away to look in the cupboards. 'Plus the nervous strain of—of all that just now.'

He braced himself. 'Let's get things out in the open, Abby. Did you push me away out of revulsion?'

She spun round to face him, shocked. 'Good heavens, no, Max.'

'Then why?' He got up and took her hands in his. 'I've had this feeling all along about you, but it wasn't a question I could ask before. Abby, is it possible that you're a virgin?'

She wrenched her hands away. 'At my age?' she said bitterly. 'Get real, Max!'

He cursed himself silently. 'I had to ask.'

'And now you know, so let's change the subject,' she said with fierce distaste.

'Right. Let's go back to the part where you were hungry,' he said quickly, but Abby shook her head.

'Oddly enough I'm not, any more. So I'd like to leave now. Better still,' she added, looking at her watch, 'if you drive me to Bristol Parkway I'll catch the next Intercity and save you the double trip.'

Max glared at her. 'To hell with that. I'll drive you back to London.'

Abby glared back, her eyes flashing gold sparks. 'No, thanks. I'd rather go by train.'

He shrugged. 'I'll wait for you in the car.'

Abby stared, deflated, as he strode out of the house and down the path. He could have tried a *bit* more persuasion, she thought furiously. She went into the kitchen and hunted out her mother's cool bag, put a loaf of bread in it from the freezer, added the eggs and milk, then collected her handbag, locked up and went to join Max in the car. With scrupulous politeness he stowed the bag in the back of the Range Rover and helped her into the passenger seat.

'Do you need directions for Bristol Parkway?' she asked coldly as he drove off.

He shook his head and switched on the CD player. 'I know this stretch of motorway like the back of my hand.'

Gianni's golden tones filled the car with liquid perfection so infinitely better than tense silence that Abby relaxed slightly as they crossed the Severn Bridge and headed for London. She forced herself to concentrate on the music, and succeeded so well that the sign for the M32 and Bristol Parkway came into view before she was ready for it.

'This is the turning!' she said frantically, but Max shook his head.

'I said I'd drive you back to London, so that's what I'll do.'

Since they were in the fast lane of a motorway jammed with traffic, Abby had no option but to sit there, fuming in frustration.

The signs for Reading came up before Max spoke again. 'Abby, listen to me. I apologise for offending you—'

'Don't bother. I prefer to forget certain aspects of today.

I'm sure you do, too.' She stared stonily ahead, and after a glance at her set profile Max kept his attention on the traffic.

When they finally reached Bayswater, after what felt like the longest journey of her life to Abby, she jumped out of the car and took the cool bag from Max. 'I know you can't hang about here, so I won't ask you in. Thank you for driving me to the party—and back,' she added. 'Even though the return journey was unnecessary. Goodbye.'

Max got back in the car without a word, and drove off without waiting until she let herself in. She trudged down to her flat, utterly crestfallen for the second time that day. She had no earthly right to feel shattered because he'd taken off like that. But she did. He could have at least said goodbye. She sniffed hard. It was obvious that Max Wingate was not a man to put up with the kind of treatment she'd meted out today. And the hell of it was she couldn't blame him. This kind of situation was depressingly familiar in her life but it hadn't mattered before, because she hadn't cared enough for the men who'd turned their backs on her in similar circumstances. But it was different with Max, she thought miserably as she put the food away. She cared a lot for him. Otherwise she would never have asked him to make love to her. Her face burned at the thought of how easily he'd seen through her. When he'd made love to her again so savagely he'd been teaching her a lesson she'd learned so rapidly that every part of her was soon on fire for him. Until the very last. But at the final hurdle she'd pushed Max away in the familiar, stupid panic that usually happened far earlier in the proceedings. She couldn't blame him for going off without a word—nor, if she were fair, for asking the hated question put to her more than once in the past.

Abby put the eggs and milk in the fridge and huddled on the sofa, too tired to move, then jumped out of her skin when the doorbell rang. *Go away, whoever you are,* she ordered wildly. But the bell rang again. And again.

'Who is it?' she snapped, snatching up the receiver.

'Who do you think?' said Max irritably. 'Buzz me in.'

Astonished, Abby did as he said. When she opened the door Max looked down at her in silence, his eyes inscrutable. Other than the hint of dark shadow on his jaw, he looked so damned immaculate, she thought resentfully, and stood aside to let him in.

'Sorry I took so long,' he said casually. 'I had a hell of a job to park.'

She stared at him, frowning. 'But why have you come back? I thought you'd be on your way down the motorway again by now.'

'Your memory needs work.' His eyes bored into hers. 'Cast your mind back. I told you I'd ignore you if you said goodbye.'

Something dead inside her came back to life. 'So you did.'

'Sit down,' he ordered curtly. 'We need to talk.'

Abby nodded meekly. Max deserved an explanation. She brightened as he took off his tie and jacket. So he wasn't leaving right away. 'Why did you come back?'

'I gave you the main reason. But I also dislike loose ends. Sit down.'

Abby sat, not sure whether she was relieved or sorry when Max chose the chair in preference to joining her on the sofa.

'You made use of me today,' he began, his saturnine cast of feature very pronounced. 'I had no objection to acting as your minder at the party. I enjoyed that. But I did object to the sexual experiment afterwards. On the journey back I had time to think. You were obviously proving something to yourself when you asked me to make love to you.'

Abby's eyes fell. 'Maybe the first time, yes,' she admitted. 'But the second time I was with you all the way until—well, until the last bit.'

'Unlike you, I'm experienced enough to know that,' he informed her, as though they were discussing some abstract problem. 'But why the desperate panic? I'm not a rapist. A simple no would have been enough.'

'I realise that, and I'm sorry.' Abby smiled wearily. 'Maybe now you can see why life is so much easier for me without a man in it.'

Max eyed her questioningly. 'Your friend's brother is obviously a lawyer of some kind, because he mentioned a possible opening in his chambers. Has he changed your mind about a job in Pennington?'

Abby shook her head. 'I still want that, even if you don't want to see me any more. Pennington's a big town. There's room for both of us.'

He frowned. 'Why wouldn't I want to see you any more?'

'After today I wouldn't blame you.'

'I don't scare so easily,' he assured her, and got up to sit beside her. 'I like a challenge. And you, Abigail Green, are very definitely a challenge. So forget about having no man in your life. I am not only in your life but I intend to stay there, whether you like it or not.'

Her mouth curved in a slow smile. 'I do like it.'

The hard eyes softened slightly. 'In that case I suggest we concentrate on getting to know each other.'

'Forget about being lovers?'

'I'm a man, so that's not easy for me.' Max took her hand in his. 'But for the time being I suggest we backtrack a bit and just enjoy each other's company.'

'I'd like that very much,' she said with relief, and smiled at him ruefully. 'Have no fear, I won't ask you to make love to me again. From now on you make the first move.'

Max grinned. 'When the time is right, you can definitely count on that!'

Abby grinned back. 'Now that's sorted I feel hungry again. Want some supper?'

A search through supplies yielded up cheese, spaghetti

and a packet of bacon, and with the addition of some of Chris Morgan's eggs Abby swiftly put together a creditable carbonara they both fell on with appetites honed by the see-saw emotions of the day.

'That was just what I needed,' said Max at last, scouring his plate with a thick slice of bread.

Abby put cheese and biscuits on the table and sat down. 'Tell me more about your job. What firm do you actually work for in Pennington?'

'My own. You may have heard of it. I set up WLS five years ago, in partnership with two fellow architects.' Max put a slice of cheese on an oatcake and crunched for a moment. 'I met Jon Stone and Harry Lucas when the three of us worked for one of the big London outfits, and eventually we decided to join forces and set up our own firm, somewhere outside the capital.'

'Why did you choose Pennington?'

'A couple of locations made the short list, but Pennington won because Jon's wife was brought up there. Harry Lucas liked it because there are excellent schools for his children, and I saw it as a place with potential for the kind of outfit I had in mind.'

'Are you the boss?' asked Abby.

He shrugged. 'I'm the senior partner, yes, but all three of us work together, with the emphasis on collaboration and flexibility. And we've been lucky enough to find a young, enthusiastic staff with the same work ethic.'

'So you're the brain behind WLS,' said Abby, impressed. 'You're right, I have heard of it. I remember the publicity when your arts centre design won all those prizes.'

Max shrugged. 'That was a big stroke of luck. I expected it to be tough to introduce modern ideas into a town where so many of the buildings date from its Regency spa days. But winning prizes with our first major design as a firm was a big boost. It brought in a lot of clients afterwards, most of whom have been very easy to work with. And in addition to big-scale projects we've done some creative extensions to several listed properties. I'll show you some of them when you come down.' He raised an eyebrow. 'When is that likely to be?'

'Soon. I've promised Simon to show my successor the ropes for a while, but after that I'll be at Briar Cottage. Mother will be back in school by then for the new term.' Abby smiled wryly. 'After complaining about seeing so little of me through the summer, she's now likely to see too much!'

Max shook his head. 'She'll be delighted to have her ewe lamb safe under her roof again.'

Abby smiled. 'But only for a while, Max. If I get a job, I'll look for a flat as soon as I can. Much as I love my mother, I'd rather rent a place of my own. I don't fancy commuting twenty country miles to work every day. But I'll enjoy being able to pop home to her whenever I get fed up with my own company,' she added with satisfaction.

'Why not look for something in my part of town?'

'Chester Gardens?' she said, eyebrows raised. 'Very smart—pricey too. No point in my looking for a flat round there.'

'I've got a spare room,' he said blandly. 'A couple of them, in fact. I could rent one to you at very reasonable terms.'

She shook her head, grinning. 'I need my space, literally and metaphorically.'

'What big words you use,' he mocked, and looked at his watch. 'Hell, it's later than I thought. I don't fancy the drive back to Pennington. I'll ring my father and stay overnight in Kew.'

Abby went with him to the door, struggling to tell him what she needed to say. Not much point in an English degree if she couldn't find the right words to let Max know how she felt. 'Thank you for today. I'm grateful.'

Max looked down at her quizzically. 'For what, exactly?'

'For the lift down—and back—in your car. For your

company at the party, and most of all for your forbearance,' she said gruffly, her eyes sliding away from his. 'I thought I'd put you off having anything more to do with me.'

He smiled indulgently. 'You still have a lot to learn about men, Abigail Green. At least about this man in particular.' He bent and kissed her cheek. 'I'll see you on Saturday about six. Think about what you'd like to do.'

Her eyes widened in delight. 'You're coming up to London again next weekend?'

Max shrugged, secretly triumphant at her reaction. 'Until you move down to my part of the world I don't have much option. In future we're going to see a lot of each other, Abigail Green. Get used to that, too.'

She smiled radiantly, feeling suddenly so light-hearted she wanted to hug him to death. 'Is that a threat or a promise?'

'Both,' he said, and gave her a swift, hard kiss. 'Sleep well.'

Two days later Isabel Green rang Abby to give her all the latest news from Venice when she reported her safe arrival home. 'Marco is gaining by the day, and Laura and Domenico have sorted the problem with Isabella so well that she now feels possessive about her little brother. "My baby", she informed me, in both languages!'

'I can just picture it.' Abby braced herself. 'Right, then, Mother dear. Now I'll give you my news.'

'What's wrong?' said Isabel in alarm.

'Nothing. You know I'm finishing work next week—'

'Have you changed your mind? Last I heard, Simon was trying to persuade you to stay on.'

'True. But I vetoed that. It's time I made a move. I've already been offered another job, in fact, but I turned it down. I'm still keen on finding something in Pennington.'

'That's a relief,' said Isabel thankfully.

'So you won't mind having me at home for a while?'

'I'll be delighted, as you well know. Though you'll find it dull here after London.'

'Not all that much, as it happens.' Abby paused. 'So, to revert to the breaking news I mentioned, I met someone when I went to Italy. In fact I took him to Rachel's engagement party. You'll probably hear all about it tomorrow.'

'I most certainly will! Is he Italian?'

'Only on the distaff side. His name is Max Wingate, and he's Giancarlo Falcone's half-brother. That's how I met him. But amazingly Max is based here in Pennington. He's the man behind WSL, the architects that won all those prizes for designing the new arts centre.'

'Really? How impressive.'

'He is, rather. Would you like to meet him some time?'

'If everyone else in Stavely has met him I most definitely would!' Isabel paused. 'Darling, how did you get on at the party?'

'Fine. I was glad I'd made the effort to go. Max made quite a hit with the locals. I took him home before we drove back and collected some milk for tea from Chris Morgan on the way. Max liked him.'

'As well he might. Did Chris like Max?'

'He asked him back to the farm any time.'

'Morgan seal of approval, then. Good. Now, I'd better ring off and let you get some sleep.'

'I'm glad you're back safe and sound. Oh, and Mother, post a *Gazette* to me, so I can comb through it for jobs.'

Abby worked hard to teach the various complexities of the job to her replacement, who proved to be such a fast learner that, with the last concert of the season under her belt, Abby worked shorter hours and got home earlier. When Sadie rang to say she fancied a girls' night out while Tom was away, Abby was all for it. It was good to spend time with someone who'd shared her Cambridge experience. But these days Sadie was a high-flyer in advertising, and she shook her head when Abby told her she was keeping to her idea of a job in Pennington.

'With your qualifications and experience—not to mention your looks, ducky—there must be loads of openings for you in London. Why on earth go back to the sticks?'

'Pennington is not the sticks, Ms Morris! I've had four years of rushing round London, remember? I need a change of pace, and a lot more time with my mother.' Abby gave her friend a crooked little grin. 'And I just happen to have met a man who runs a company based in Pennington.'

'Have you, indeed?' Sadie settled back in her chair, dark eyes gleaming. 'Tell Auntie Sadie all about it. Every last detail.'

Sadie Morris had been a kindred spirit since their first meeting at Trinity, and Abby was only too pleased to tell, if not every last detail, at least enough about Max to keep Sadie hanging on to every word, entranced.

'Running into Mr Right up a mountain in Umbria—how romantic is that? Is he gorgeous, then?'

Abby felt her usual frisson of reaction as she thought of Max's dark, heavy-lidded eyes and the tall, muscular body that roused such surprising responses in her own. '*I* think he is.'

'Then he must be *über*-gorgeous. Admit it, you've fallen at last,' crowed Sadie. 'Well, well, Miss Cool. Welcome to the club. I knew you'd join us one day.'

CHAPTER SIX

WHEN Max arrived the following Saturday, Abby was so glad to see him she threw herself into his arms, and he promptly swept her off her feet, his mouth on hers and his arms cracking her ribs before he'd even kicked her door shut behind him.

'I've missed you,' he said tersely, when he set her down.

'Likewise,' she said breathlessly. 'What shall we do this evening?'

'Other than go straight to bed and make mad, passionate love?' he said, only half joking.

'Other than that,' she agreed regretfully.

'I'm taking you out to dinner,' he announced.

'Smart or casual?'

'Just the way you are.'

'Are you serious?' Abby gave a disparaging glance at her jeans and plain white T-shirt. 'These are staying-in clothes. I waited until you came before I changed because I wasn't sure what you had in mind.'

Just as well, thought Max wryly. When he was away from her it was possible—just—to be patient and give her all the time she needed to get used to the idea of them as lovers. But after a week apart her spontaneous greeting sent his high-minded ideas right out of the window. 'Don't change. You look perfect,' he assured her. 'We have time before we leave. I don't suppose you'd have a beer?'

She smiled triumphantly. 'I went shopping this morning.'

Max put his arm round her and led her to the sofa. 'So tell me what you've been doing all week.'

'I do that every night when you ring me.'

'You weren't in last night,' he reminded her. 'I had to leave a message.'

'I was out carousing with Sadie Morris, the friend who used to live here with me. Her man was away, so we had a girls' night out.'

Max eyed her with interest. 'Exactly what do "girls" talk about on such occasions?'

'Men,' said Abby promptly. 'You, specifically.'

His eyes narrowed. 'What did you say?'

'I described the way we met and what you do for a living.' She gave him a feline little smile. 'Sadie asked if you were gorgeous.'

Max drank down some of his beer, his eyes on hers over the rim of the glass. 'And what was your answer to that?'

'I said I certainly thought so.'

Max put down his glass, took her wine glass away from her and hauled her onto his lap. 'If you say things like that you run certain risks,' he said roughly, and kissed her until her head reeled.

'You haven't gone off me, then?' she gasped when she could speak.

'Does it look like it?'

She smiled at him smugly. 'No. Do we have to go out? I could cook you something.'

'In case you hadn't noticed, I'm human, Abigail Green, so we go out.' Max put her back in her corner, and drained his glass. 'Dinner is at eight.'

'In that case I'd better change,' she said, frowning down

at her T-shirt, which no longer looked pristine after Max's attentions.

'If you must,' he said, resigned. 'How about that dress you wore in Todi?'

'It's nothing special,' she said doubtfully.

'It looked special to me.' He got up and hauled her to her feet. 'Off you go, then, and don't take long.'

Abby shut her bedroom door behind her and peeled off her shirt and jeans, then paused as she passed the full-length mirror set in the wardrobe door. She stripped off her underwear and stood looking at herself objectively, trying to see her naked body with Max's eyes. She lacked Sadie's voluptuous curves above the waist, but knew Sadie would have sold her soul for the narrow hips and long legs she herself took for granted. Not bad, decided Abby. She put on underwear kept for special occasions and studied herself again. Better. The bra pushed her breasts up a bit, and the knickers were the kind meant to be taken off by a man the instant he clapped eyes on them, according to Sadie, who had given her the set for her birthday. Abby slid the simple black dress over her head, hung her amber drops in her ears, replaced the lipstick Max had put paid to and went for gold sandals in preference to black killer heels. If he wanted her exactly as she'd looked in Todi, she might as well go the whole hog.

She put a lacy black cardigan over her arm and joined Max. He got to his feet like a panther ready to pounce, a look in his eyes that made her wonder if he could see through her dress.

'You look sensational,' he said huskily.

'Thank you,' she said, backing away hastily. 'Don't kiss me or I'll have to start all over again.'

'How do you know I want to kiss you?'

'I just do. Is it time to go?'

'Yes, otherwise I most certainly will kiss you, and you *will* have to start over again,' he assured her.

Outside Max flagged down a taxi straight away, for which Abby was grateful. There was an autumnal feel to the evening, and her cardigan was for show rather than warmth. He gave the driver the address and drew Abby close.

'You're shivering,' he said, concerned.

'Cuddle me, then.'

Abby felt deliciously comfortable held close to Max, breathing in the familiar man and soap scent of him, and became so involved in catching up on their week apart that she forgot to ask where they were heading until they hit the Hammersmith roundabout.

'This is a long way to get something to eat,' she commented. 'Where's the restaurant?'

'It's a surprise,' he said, but remained impervious to her coaxing until they arrived in a quiet side-road not far from Kew Gardens.

Abby gave Max a startled look as they walked up a short path to a large house shielded from its neighbours by high laurel hedges either side. When Max pressed the brass bell on the open outer door, the inner stained-glass door opened almost immediately to reveal a slim, silver-haired man in a striped butcher's apron. He smiled at them in warm welcome as he beckoned them inside with a wooden spoon.

'Meet the chef,' said Max, grinning.

'I'm David Wingate, and you, I know, are Miss Abigail Green,' said his father, with a reproving look at his son as he took her hand. 'Welcome, my dear. But you'll have to come straight to the kitchen. I'm at a critical stage.'

'How do you do?' said Abby, shooting a wild look of reproach at Max.

'Abby thought I was taking her to a restaurant, Dad,' he explained as they followed his father down the black and white diamond tiles of the hall into a big, brightly lit kitchen with an impressive array of cooking utensils hanging from a rack over a central island.

David Wingate smiled kindly at Abby. 'Perhaps he was afraid you wouldn't come if it meant meeting his father.'

She shook her head. 'Absolutely not, Mr Wingate. I'm very glad to meet you. Forgive my surprise.'

David took a leisurely look at her under the bright lights. 'I rather fancy it would be easy to forgive you anything, Abigail.'

'She prefers Abby,' Max informed him, and leaned against the island. 'What's cooking, Dad?'

'Nothing fancy. Just a plump chicken that grew up happy. I was about to make gravy. Give Abby a glass of wine.' David smiled at her. 'Max says you like yours white and dry.'

'I do. Thank you.' She hesitated. 'I'd like to help. May I?'

He looked pleased. 'Why not? Max, find her an apron to tie over that delightful dress.'

Max took her small black bag and cardigan, unhooked another striped apron from a peg and wrapped Abby in it. 'There you go.'

'Shall I make the gravy? I usually do for my mother,' she told David.

'Then you shall for us,' he said promptly. 'Max, you can finish laying the table in the dining room.'

'I do old-fashioned gravy,' warned Abby.

'The best kind,' said David, pushing the roasting tin along the hotplate. 'I've already drained off the excess fat and made up some chicken stock—dare I hope that you're going to use flour?'

'Of course,' she said, smiling. 'Plus the other ingredient my mother considers vital—patience.'

Any constraint Abby had felt at meeting Max's father vanished as they worked together. While she concentrated on the gravy, David drained vegetables and put them in the warming oven with the herb-stuffed chicken, which Abby told him smelt heavenly.

David smiled, pleased, and confided that he'd heard all about her dramatic meeting with his son.

'He was really hacked off with me, Mr Wingate.' Abby grinned at him, then tasted a teaspoonful of the gravy, added a grind of salt and pepper and set the pan on the back of the stove to keep warm.

'Call me David,' he said casually. 'Max speaks very good Italian, of course.'

'Like a native. My brother-in-law's Italian, so I'm in a position to judge. Though Domenico's from Venice, so the accent's a bit different.'

'Max spoke it before English. He told you his mother is Italian?'

Abby nodded. 'And you probably know I've met Gianni. I was on my way to sign him up for some concerts when I ran into Max.'

'The table's done, Dad,' said Max as he came in. 'Shall I take in the first course?'

David looked undecided. 'Now I've met Abby, I realise we could have eaten less formally in the kitchen.'

'True. Formal females don't make gravy the minute they're through the door,' agreed Max. 'No problem. I'll cart everything back out here and we can eat at the break-fast table.'

In response to questions from both men Abby described her job over melon with shavings of Parma ham, and told anec-dotes about the various artists she'd met during her time as Simon Hadley's assistant.

'But I've persuaded Abby to look for work in Pennington now she's resigned,' said Max.

'You'll miss the excitement and variety,' said his father.

'I will,' she admitted. 'But I certainly won't miss the crises that boil up when temperaments clash.'

'One thing you can say for Gianni,' said Max. 'He's not

temperamental in the slightest. At least not yet. You sit there,' he added. 'I'll help Dad.'

'How did the concert in Rome go?' said David. He decanted the gravy into a sauceboat then set a crisp, golden chicken down in front of Max.

'A triumph, apparently. He's already rehearsing for a Christmas special.' Max began carving succulent slices while his father helped Abby to potatoes and runner beans, both of which he informed her with endearing pride were grown in the garden at the back of the house.

'My vegetable plot is small but gratifyingly productive,' said David, handing her the gravy boat. 'Since I retired I enjoy gardening. I sit glued to TV gardening programmes. Though my own father,' he added, 'managed perfectly well without their help. Due to his efforts the garden has always been in good heart. Excellent gravy, my dear,' he added. 'Try some, Max.'

Max not only tried some, but finished it all off and went to the stove to get the rest from the pot. 'I hope you weren't counting on any for tomorrow, Dad.'

Abby smiled at him, thanking him with her eyes for his compliment. 'How long has your family lived in this house?' she asked, turning to David.

'My father brought my mother to it as a bride, but she died when I was a child, so it's been a very masculine household for most of its history.' He exchanged a glance with Max. 'My wife didn't live here long, either. She was constantly homesick for her native Umbria.'

'Not any more,' said Max dryly. 'These days she prefers Venice.'

'True.' David smiled at Abby. 'Tell me about your relatives in Venice. Max says you were there recently.'

Abby was only too happy to talk about the new baby, and his gorgeous little sister. 'Domenico runs the Forli Palace Hotel, but their private home is an apartment in San Marco.

It's too small since Baby Marco arrived, so Domenico's in the process of acquiring a courtyard apartment with more rooms.'

'Is he selling the other one?' asked Max.

'No.' Abby smiled a little. 'It's where he lived when he first met Laura, and they both have a sentimental attachment to it. Domenico's going to make it earn its keep by letting it out, but with certain times of the year left free so my mother and I can use it. Domenico's parents prefer his private apartment in the hotel.'

'Does your sister get homesick?' asked David.

'I'm sure she does now and then, but Domenico's a very caring husband. So this year they're spending Christmas in Stavely.'

'It's going to be a tight fit for six of you at Briar Cottage,' commented Max.

Abby nodded ruefully. 'So I'd better get on with finding a place in Pennington to relieve the congestion.'

She regretfully refused seconds, and felt grateful she had when David brought out the pudding.

'Which you must eat, because I grow these too,' he said, and put a glass bowl of perfect raspberries on the table with a jug of cream.

Abby had truly believed she couldn't eat another thing, but the first taste of the perfumed fruit roused her tastebuds, and she ate her share, cream and all, with relish much appreciated by her host.

'Take Abby into the sitting room, Max,' David instructed. 'I'll make coffee.'

The spacious room at the front of the house was high-ceilinged and furnished with a harmonious mélange of antiques and contemporary comfort, but Abby had no time to look at it. The moment they were through the door, Max closed it and took her into his arms, kissing her with even more hunger than he'd displayed for his dinner.

'I needed that,' he said, releasing her, and smiled smugly as he handed over her bag. 'I knew you'd want to make repairs.'

'You planned this in advance,' she accused breathlessly, and went over to the triple mirror over the fireplace to mend the damage.

'I haven't seen you for a week,' he pointed out. 'All through dinner I had one idea in mind—to get you alone so I could kiss you senseless.'

Abby squeezed his hand and led him over to an array of photographs on a small escritoire, her throat tightening at the sight of Max as a little boy holding the hand of a stunningly beautiful woman. She turned to look at him. 'Is this your mother?'

He nodded. 'That's Luisa.'

'She was so young,' said Abby, surprised, and eyed the girlish face closely. 'You look just like her. Far more than Gianni does.'

'His hair and eyes come from Enzo, who was movie-star handsome. But the bone structure and the eyebrows are Luisa's.'

'And yours.'

'And mine,' he agreed.

'Luisa was barely eighteen when you were born. Far too young,' said his father, coming in with a tray. 'But she was clever enough to produce a son who was a carbon copy of herself. People used to remark on it when they saw them together.'

'The only time I spent away from her was with Mrs Potter, who made the cakes and cooked for Grandpa. Luisa,' he explained, 'is great with sauces and pasta and traditional Italian fare, but Grandpa insisted on a plain meat-and-potato kind of diet.'

'He wouldn't even taste the food Luisa cooked,' said David, pouring coffee. 'So after a while she just cooked for Max and herself when I was out and left the rest to Mrs Potter.' He gave Abby a straight look. 'You must be wondering how on earth a homesick teenager from Umbria came here to live with me in Kew.'

'I am,' admitted Abby honestly, 'but please don't feel you have to explain.'

'It's no secret,' he assured her, handing her a cup.

'Dad had just started teaching Italian and French at the college. Luisa worked in her uncle's restaurant nearby,' said Max. 'I was an accident.'

Abby flushed scarlet, and shot a reproachful look at him.

'He's right, of course,' said David, unruffled. 'When Luisa told me she was pregnant we got married right away. But because the knot was tied by a registrar instead of a Catholic priest I believe she never really felt married to me.'

Abby was beginning to feel far more sympathy with Luisa than she'd expected to. This was a quiet house in a very quiet part of Kew, and with only an elderly man and the cook for company during the day life would have been pretty dull for a teenage girl from such a different background.

'It wasn't so widely diagnosed in those days, but with hindsight I realise that Luisa suffered from severe post-natal depression for some time after Max's birth,' said David ruefully. 'I took her back home to Todi whenever I could, but it wasn't possible very often, both financially and due to my job. She found it harder and harder to come back every time. Looking back, it's surprising she stuck it out here as long as she did.'

Max took Abby's cup to refill it. 'If she hadn't been terrified of flying alone I suppose she'd have taken off sooner.'

'When her mother was ill she begged me to let her take you with her that last time,' said his father. 'But I wouldn't hear of it in term time when you were doing so well in school.'

'If she had taken me and wanted to keep me there would you have agreed?' asked Max.

'No,' said his father flatly. 'If my wife wished to leave me

I had no choice but to let her go. But no way would I have parted with my son.' He turned to smile at Abby. 'We must be embarrassing you with all this old family history, but Max insisted that you should hear it.'

'Thank you for telling me,' said Abby, wondering exactly why Max had wanted her to know. She got up to put her coffee cup on the tray. 'May I look at the other photographs?'

Max stood over the display with her, identifying the subjects. 'The stern gentleman in the panama hat with a watch chain across his chest is my grandfather. That's me, scowling, on his knee.'

'You were very cute,' said Abby, grinning at him. 'Is the lady in the flowered apron Mrs Potter?'

'That's the one. The rest are all me. Cricket eleven, rugby fifteen and so on.'

'And here you are in mortar-board and gown.' The stern young graduate stared unsmiling from the photograph, the slanting brows and firmly clenched mouth already displaying the saturnine look Max was wearing right that minute, she saw when she looked at him. 'You were a good-looking lad,' she said, then noticed a photograph taken about the same time, but he was smiling, in casual clothes in bright sunlight. A strikingly handsome man stood with one arm round the shoulders of Gianni, aged eleven or so, the other round Max.

'Enzo Falcone,' said David, looking over her shoulder. 'The childhood sweetheart Luisa met up with again the very day she returned to Todi, so it's no surprise that she never came back. Charming fellow, though. I liked him.'

Max turned away abruptly. 'Show Abby your music collection, Dad.'

David led her to an impressive array of compact discs, confessing that his taste leaned towards male vocal, in particular Placido Domingo and Bryn Terfel. But he also owned everything Gianni had recorded so far.

'That boy's going far, Abby,' he said with certainty.

'I agree. Will you come to one of his concerts next year?'

'Of course. If I get a hamper from Fortnums, will you join me in a picnic?'

'I'd be delighted.'

'Hey,' said Max, 'are you trying to lure my woman away from me?'

His father grinned. 'She makes such delicious gravy, who could blame me?'

'Did you enjoy the evening once you got over the surprise?' Max asked on the way back.

Abby nodded fervently. 'Of course I did. Your father's a real charmer. Though I'm surprised—and flattered—that he talked about his marriage to a complete stranger.'

'Purely because I asked him to. He was doubtful before-hand, but he took to you on sight or he wouldn't have said a word. Besides, I gave him a very pertinent piece of information before he even set eyes on you.'

Abby looked up at him curiously. 'And what was that?'

'It was about our meeting on my famous road. You told me afterwards that I looked familiar, but that, of course, was because you'd seen photographs of Gianni.' Max's arm tightened round her. 'Once I'd recovered from the shock of almost killing you, I recognised you right away, Abby.'

'But you'd never met me before,' she said blankly.

'True. But I knew right away who you were. There was a sticky moment when I mistook you for one of Gianni's groupies—ouch, that hurt,' he complained as she jabbed him in the ribs with an elbow. He took in a deep breath. 'I am trying to say something very profound here, Abigail Green.'

'Sorry. Do go on.'

'Before I came to fetch you this evening I told my father that when I'd calmed down enough to take a good look at you that day a voice in my head said, "Wake up, Wingate. Here she is. At last".'

Abby twisted round to look up at him, her eyes wide in the semi-darkness of the cab. He smiled down at her.

'Maybe I should wait until we get to your place before I say any more.'

'No. Tell me now.'

'You're the woman I've been waiting for all my adult life.' Max bent his head to plant a kiss on her parted mouth. 'Abigail Green, I want you for keeps.'

CHAPTER SEVEN

MAX STOOD with his back to the closed door of Abby's flat, arms folded. 'I've obviously deprived you of speech.'

She swallowed hard. 'I thought we were going to take time, just concentrate on being friends for a while.'

His eyes hardened. 'Which is a pretty clear indication of your response.'

She flung out a hand in appeal. 'Max, please.'

'Please what, Abby?'

'Please sit down and listen to me?'

He looked at her for a long moment, then crossed the room to sit at one end of the sofa. Taking this as a good sign, she sat beside him.

'I'm listening,' he prompted.

Lord, this was difficult. Abby took in a deep breath, choosing her words with care. 'If we had a permanent relationship of some kind you would naturally expect us to be lovers,' she said at last, staring at the pink polish on her toenails, the pattern in the carpet—anywhere but at Max.

'A reasonable assumption,' he agreed dryly.

'Of course it is.' She swallowed. 'But even though I'm in love with you that might never be possible.'

From the corner of her eye she saw him tense at the

mention of love. He moved nearer and turned her face towards him. 'Why not?'

Colour flared in her face. 'Because I'm so utterly hopeless at sex.'

He took her hand in his and sat back, careful to make no other contact. 'When we were together at Briar Cottage you seemed happy with it up to a point.'

'I was—deliriously. That's why I'm trying to be straight with you, Max. No other man has ever made me feel remotely like that. Normally I can't even get beyond the kissing stage without panicking.' She heaved a sigh. 'With you I really thought it would happen at last. That's why I tried to—well, to seduce you. But I was hopeless at that, too.'

'I wouldn't say that. It worked rather well,' he said dryly. 'Have you tried seducing anyone before?'

She gave him a scathing glance. 'Be serious! I tried with you because I actually wanted you to make love to me.'

'But when it came to the crunch you still couldn't go through with it. Even though,' he added without inflection, 'you say you're in love with me. Is that the truth?'

'Yes, Max. I may have problems with sex but I don't lie!' She sat with shoulders hunched. 'That's what's so depressing.'

His lips twitched. 'Depressing?'

'If I can't make love with you I never will with anyone. Not that I want to. With anyone, I mean—you know what I mean!'

'I get the drift.' Max put a careful arm round Abby's waist, paused to gauge her reaction, and when she made no move to pull away drew her close. 'You obviously had a bad experience some time. I've already asked one painful question, but—'

'You don't need to ask the other one,' she said, resigned. 'I know what you're going to say. It wasn't rape.' She felt him relax slightly. 'But I wasn't really a willing partner in the procedure either, so it hurt, and put me off the idea altogether. The boy was astounded when he found it was my first time, but by then he couldn't stop. He was desperately apologetic afterwards.'

'A bit late for that,' said Max savagely. 'I suppose he went merrily on his way afterwards with no idea of the damage he'd done.' He frowned. 'But what happened when you were let loose in a crowd of randy undergraduates at Trinity? How the devil did you cope there?'

'I had a stroke of luck. I met Sadie the moment I arrived. We were kindred spirits from day one, so I asked her help with my little problem. She was a year older than me in actual time, but light years older in other ways. Her advice was simple. I should just tell everyone that the love of my life was waiting for me back home. It worked. Almost from the first, Sadie and I were part of a group that did most things together. The others had taken a year off before going up to Trinity so I was the youngest and they were protective towards me—like you.' Abby smiled ruefully. 'I had such a good time there, Max. I enjoyed every minute of it, work and play. But afterwards, when I came to London, I decided it was time to start acting like an adult and say yes when men asked me out. And ran head-on into the problem again. Not every man tried to get to first base right away, of course, so occasionally I went out with someone a couple of times before the inevitable happened. As it did in the end with Silas, as you've probably guessed.' She looked at him in appeal. 'You can see now why life's so much easier with no man in it. I want *you* in my life very much, but now you know about my problem, Max Wingate, are you sure you want me in yours?'

'Good God, of course I am,' he said, so matter-of-factly she could have hugged him. 'No problem is insoluble.'

Abby eyed him challengingly. 'How do you intend to solve mine?'

He grinned. 'The same way you make gravy—with expertise and patience.'

She let out a deep breath and smiled back. 'Thank you, Max. I'll try hard not to tax your patience too far.'

He shook his head firmly. 'No trying required. One day the problem will solve itself.'

'What do we do until then?'

'Take things one day at a time. First of all I'd like to meet your mother, and get her used to the idea that I'm a fixture in your life.' Max put a finger under her chin and turned her face up to his. 'Secondly, I can't promise not to make love to you. *Love*, Abby, not sex. I can take, and hopefully give, infinite pleasure in kissing and caressing you without trying to stampede you into the final act. This obviously causes the panic, so we won't go there until you're ready.'

'What if I'm never ready?'

'Never is a long time,' he said and looked deep into her eyes. 'The one constant thing you must keep in mind is that I love you. All of you. The heart and mind and character, as well as the beautiful packaging—though I'm pretty delighted with that too.'

Abby slid her arms round Max's neck and kissed him back in passionate gratitude. 'I love all those integral parts of you, too, Max Wingate.' She smiled suddenly. 'Impressive packaging included.'

He held her close and buried his face in her hair, his heart beating strongly in time with hers. 'Now that's settled, will you marry me, Abigail Green?'

She took in a deep, shaky breath. 'I want to so much it frightens me, but are you sure it's worth the risk? In the circumstances, I mean?'

Max raised his head, his smile so tender her heart turned over. 'Circumstances change, my darling. And as long as you love me even half as much as I love you the outcome is guaranteed. So do I take that as a yes?'

Abby looked at him for a long, tense moment then nodded. 'Yes,' she said fiercely. 'You do.'

* * *

Abby spent another evening with Sadie during the week, joined her colleagues for a farewell lunch on the Friday, then spent the rest of the day packing, ready to stow her possessions in Max's car the following afternoon.

'You're actually taking him home to meet Mother?' asked Laura during their weekly telephone call.

'It's pretty vital that I do, because I've met his father already,' said Abby, and described the evening with David Wingate.

'This is serious stuff, then?'

'If you're asking if I'm in love with him, the answer's yes.'

'Wow! I'm dying to meet this Max of yours. So is Domenico.'

'When you've moved to the new apartment maybe I'll bring him to see you.'

'No maybe about it. We both need to check that this man is good enough for you!'

'I told her you were,' she informed Max, when he arrived to collect her the following day.

He kissed her again. 'Thank you. I'll do my best to prove you right.' He looked at the luggage and boxes piled in the living room. 'Is this the lot?'

'Everything I own.'

'Then lock up and let's get a move on. I'm parked on a double yellow line.'

As Abby locked the flat door for the last time she felt as though she were locking away a chapter in her life, but any slight pang of regret was quickly dispelled by the sheer pleasure of being with Max again as they set off.

'Just listen to me!' she said at one stage on the journey. 'I've hardly let you get a word in. What's the news on Gianni?'

'Much to his agent's delight, he's besieged with offers of work after the television concert, including a new recording contract.'

'I'm glad about Gianni's success, but I actually meant his love-life.'

Max grinned. 'He seems pretty happy about that, too—probably because Luisa's safe in Venice. To keep her happy he went to stay with her there for a day or two after the concert in Rome, but he's back at the Villa Falcone right now, officially to rehearse but also to pursue his love affair with Signorina X until his next engagement.'

'Still no clue as to who she is?'

'No. Gianni assured me that she's single, with no jealous *fidanzato* hovering, knife at the ready, but he still wouldn't give me a name.' Max shook his head, smiling. 'Stubborn young mule. If he's serious about the girl he'll have to go public some time. I told him about you, by the way. He's delighted with the idea of you as his *cognata*.'

Abby blinked. 'That's jumping the gun a bit. I'm not Gianni's sister-in-law yet.'

'So you do know some Italian, then!'

'When spoken at a reasonable speed by someone who's not furious with me, I can manage a few words.'

'Tell me you love me, then.'

She smiled. *'Ti amo, Massimo.'*

'Do you, my darling?' he said, in a tone that melted her into a puddle.

'You should know I do by now,' she said huskily, and sighed. 'Actually, I meant to show you how much after you took me home from Kew last week. I even changed into sexy underwear for the occasion. But when you started talking marriage it went clean out of my head. I forgot all about my seduction plan until I got undressed that night.'

Max let out a crack of laughter as he tried to keep his attention on the traffic. 'It just slipped your mind?'

Abby pulled a face. 'I told you I was hopeless at that kind of thing.'

He put out a hand to touch her knee. 'Forget the plans, Abby. Let nature take its course. Which it will, one day, because it always does.'

'By then maybe you'll have given up on me,' she said forlornly.

'That,' he said with emphasis, 'will never happen.'

Isabel Green was dead-heading a few surviving roses in the front garden when they arrived, her short blonde hair ruffled by the late-afternoon breeze. Trim in eggshell-blue sweater and tailored grey trousers, she came smiling to meet them, and as soon as the Range Rover came to a stop in the lane beside the cottage Abby jumped out and ran to hug her mother.

'Hi. You look good, Mrs Green. This is Max Wingate,' she said, smiling at him as he came through the gate, laden with luggage.

Isabel held out her hand. 'How do you do, Mr Wingate? I would say welcome to Briar Cottage, but Abby tells me you've been here already.'

'We called in on the day of her friend's party, long enough to admire your garden. I'm very happy to meet you, Mrs Green.' He put down his load and shook her hand formally. 'Even happier,' he added, smiling, 'if you'll call me Max.'

'Then I shall,' she said promptly. 'Come in and have a drink.'

'We'd better get my stuff out of the way first,' said Abby. 'Some of it will have to overflow into Laura's room until I decide what to do with it.'

'Put everything in there for now, darling. You can transfer things at your leisure tomorrow.'

Max insisted on doing it all, and made short work of carrying luggage and boxes upstairs. When everything was stacked neatly in Laura's room he made a detour to the bathroom to wash while Abby ran down to her mother in the kitchen.

'Well?' she demanded in a fierce whisper. 'Do you like him?'

Isabel smiled. 'You want me to like him?'

'Yes.' Two pairs of identical eyes met and held. 'Because I'm very much in love with him. In fact, Mother—'

Footsteps on the stairs prevented her from saying more. Abby smiled as Max appeared in the kitchen doorway. 'Ready for that drink?'

Isabel suggested they sit outside. 'It's still quite warm for the time of year. If you'd prefer a beer to wine, Max, I left some in the fridge.'

'I'll bring it,' said Abby, and followed the others outside to watch the sun set over the perfectly kept garden.

'Abby says you do all this yourself, Mrs Green,' said Max.

Isabel smiled. 'Not these days. I get help once a week, sometimes more, but I still do as much as I can.'

Abby's eyebrows rose. 'Who did you find, Mother?'

'Someone at the Garden Club recommended a garden services firm, and they're very good.' Isabel smiled at Max. 'I hear that your first meeting with my daughter was memorable.'

'You could certainly say that,' he agreed, exchanging a grin with Abby. 'When you go to Venice next you should take a leaf out of Abby's book and make a detour to Todi. You could stay at my house.'

'As long as someone else drives you there,' said Abby wryly. 'The view is spectacular and the house is beautiful—Max designed it himself. But the approach to it is not for the faint-hearted.'

'It's easier by the back road,' said Max. 'Next time you come I'll drive you up that way.'

'I've never been to Umbria,' Isabel confessed. 'In fact, until Laura married Domenico, I'd never been to Italy at all.'

'Todi's very different from Venice,' said Abby. 'But just as beautiful in its own way—the architecture's ravishing. I loved it. We had pasta with truffles for dinner there. Talking of food, something smells wonderful in the kitchen. Can we eat soon?'

'Abby said she had a delicious meal with your father, Max,' Isabel said as they went inside. 'He enjoys cooking?'

'It's something he's taken to in a big way now he's retired—the garden too.' Max smiled affectionately. 'He boasted about his home-grown vegetables to Abby.'

'Is your father enjoying his retirement?' asked Isabel. 'This isn't an idle question,' she added wryly. 'I'll be enjoying mine soon. At least I hope so. Right now I have serious qualms about it. I just can't visualise life as a lady of leisure.'

'Dad seems to find plenty to do. And he travels quite a lot.'

'Sensible man,' said Isabel, putting a joint of hot glazed ham on the table.

'Would you care to do the honours? I can manage perfectly well if not, but some men are unnerved by the sight of a woman with a carving knife in her hand.'

'Not me,' said Max, laughing. 'But I'm happy to carve for you. This smells wonderful.'

The ham was accompanied by a platter of crisp roasted vegetables and hot damson sauce, and Max ate two helpings of everything. 'I hope you taught Abby to cook like this,' he said fervently.

Isabel gave him a straight look. 'Are her cooking skills likely to feature much in your life, then, Max?'

'My mother tends not to beat about the bush,' warned Abby, grinning.

'Then I won't either,' said Max, suddenly sober as he held Isabel's eyes. 'I love your daughter, Mrs Green, regardless of whether she can cook. I was going to lead up to this rather more subtly, but I'm hoping you'll give me your blessing anyway. I've asked your beautiful daughter to marry me, and she's said yes.'

Isabel's eyes widened, then she smiled in delight and jumped up to embrace her daughter. 'You never said a word, darling.'

'I did. I told you I was in love with him!'

'True,' allowed Isabel, 'and that was surprise enough. But I didn't realise things had progressed so far.'

'I knew what I wanted the moment I set eyes on Abby,' said Max, and got to his feet, eyeing Isabel steadily. 'Are you willing to give her to me, Mrs Green?'

'I'm not a pound of tea,' teased Abby, but her eyes were wet.

Isabel turned from her daughter's glowing face to meet the dark, compelling eyes trained on her own. 'If Abby loves you enough to want to marry you I'm very happy to give my blessing. We've only just met, Max, but my instinct tells me you'll take care of her.'

'I will. Always,' he said without drama.

'In that case,' said his future mother-in-law, 'you'd better call me Isabel.' She smiled on them both and raised her wine glass in toast. 'To your present and future happiness.'

'Amen to that,' said Max with feeling, and kissed Abby fleetingly before raising his glass to his lips.

With that hurdle safely over, the rest of Max's visit passed in a daze of happiness for Abby. When the meal was cleared away, and they were sitting in the other room over coffee, she laughed when her mother brought out a packet of photographs.

'And now,' announced Isabel, 'I'm going to don my "grandma" hat and bore you rigid, Max. I brought these back from Venice and depend on you to ooh and ahh in all the right places.'

Max obediently made suitable comments when the photographs of the Chiesa son and heir were presented to him. 'I don't know much about babies, but he's a very handsome specimen.'

'How about his sister, then?' said Abby, handing him a photograph of Isabella in the frilly white dress bought for the christening.

Max whistled as he looked at the enchanting blonde two-year-old. Her big blue eyes shone with love as she smiled for the camera. 'What a charmer! Who was the photographer?'

'Her beloved Papa, as you can tell by the look on her face.

This,' Abby added, sliding another snap in front of him, 'is the full set. Domenico and Laura, with Isabella between them clutching the baby.'

'It's easy to see where Isabella gets her looks. Her father's going to have some headaches when she grows up.' Max looked from Laura's smiling face to Abby and shook his head in wonder. 'Bringing up such beautiful daughters must have given you a few scary moments along the way, Isabel.'

'You could say that,' she agreed with feeling. 'I find life far more restful as a grandmother. I adore my grandchildren, but after enjoying myself with them I can hand them back to their parents—the perfect arrangement.'

When Max got up to go, he suggested that Isabel might like to come to lunch in his house in Pennington with Abby next day, but she shook her head.

'That's very kind of you, but I already have an invitation to Sunday lunch. I took it for granted that Abby would be spending the day with you tomorrow.'

'Anyone I know?' asked Abby.

'The new people at Down End.' Isabel smiled at Max. 'I shall now go up and watch television in my room so you can have some time to yourselves. Stay as long as you like, Max, it's early yet.'

'Does that mean you approve?' he asked bluntly.

'Yes, I do,' she said, equally bluntly, and Max grinned and bent to kiss her cheek.

'Thank you. Thank you for dinner, too. Next time,' he added, waving a disparaging hand at the jeans worn to deal with Abby's possessions, 'I'll wear clothes more worthy of the cuisine.'

Abby kissed her mother goodnight, then sat down on the sofa with Max. 'That went well,' she said happily.

He pulled her close. 'Have you brought anyone here before?'

'Not in the way you mean. A couple of blokes from Cardiff

were happy to give me a lift from college on the way home now and then, because Mother always fed them. Sadie used to come and stay, too. She loves it here.'

'I can see why.' Max smiled at her. 'Dad's keen to meet your mother some time. He suggested I drive you both up to Kew for lunch one Sunday. How would Isabel feel about that?'

'She'd probably like that very much.' Abby gave him a troubled look.

'What's troubling you, my darling?'

She shook her head. 'However much I want to marry you, I won't do it until I've managed to slay my particular dragon first.'

'I'm happy to assist you with that any time.'

'I'm not joking!'

'Neither am I.' He kissed her fleetingly. 'Relax, Abby. No one's pushing you into anything other than a visit to my house tomorrow.'

'Is that where we'd live if—?'

'*When* we get married, not if,' he corrected.

She heaved a sigh. 'Maybe we should just live together, Max. It would make things a lot easier.'

'Easier to slay your dragon?'

'No, to end things if I don't.'

He turned her face up to his. 'Have you always been such a pessimist?'

She shrugged. 'I think of myself as a realist.'

'Does your mother know about your problem?'

'She knows about the original fiasco, yes, but not the knock-on effect it's had on me since.'

'Then you should talk it over with her.'

Abby eyed him askance. 'Are you serious? I could no more talk about my sex-life with Mother than ask about hers. Not that she has one.'

'How do you know?' Max smiled at her. 'Your mother is a very attractive lady, Abigail Green.'

'I'd just never thought—'

'That your mother could be involved with a man in that way?'

'Or any way at all,' she admitted reluctantly.

'I'm damned sure my father hasn't lived like a monk all these years—nor does the idea bother me in the slightest.'

'Has he ever brought someone home to the house in Kew?'

'Not while I've been there. But I left home years ago.' Max grinned. 'Dad could have a harem for all I know.'

'Which makes my point! You've never discussed it with him.'

He threw up a hand in defeat. 'All right. We'll cross Isabel off the list. How about your sister?'

Abby shook her head. 'I could talk to Laura about it, but I'd have to ask her not to tell Domenico, and that wouldn't be fair.'

'So it's just you and me, babe.' Max kissed her gently, and then not so gently. Abby's lips parted and he held her close, his lips and caressing hands increasingly urgent as she responded to him with fervour which escalated so quickly his self-control soon hung by a thread.

'This isn't fair, either,' he growled, but she wriggled closer, and locked her hands round his neck.

'It's lovely, though,' she whispered, her breath hot against his ear, and she trembled as she felt a shudder run through the hard body pressed against hers.

'You're turned on by the risk of discovery,' he accused, and yanked her sweater down and put her back on the sofa beside him.

Abby struggled for breath. 'You're probably right. Why can't I feel like that when we're alone, Max?'

'You will,' he promised, and held out a hand to pull her to her feet.

'There's one consolation,' she said as he pulled on his leather jacket. 'I've never felt remotely like that with anyone else.'

'Of course you haven't.' He smoothed her hair back from her face. 'You didn't care a toss for any of the others.'

'True,' she agreed, and smiled with such radiance he blinked. 'Whereas I love you madly, Max Wingate.'

He seized her by the shoulders. 'Will you repeat that tomorrow when we're alone?'

'If I do, what will happen?'

'Try it and find out!'

In common with many other houses in the town, Max Wingate's home dated from the early nineteenth century, with a wrought-iron balcony and multi-paned windows set flat in its pale walls. Outside it was pure Regency, but the interior had none of the austerity Abby had pictured.

'I thought it would be all minimal and male,' she told him as she inspected rooms furnished in almost sybaritic comfort.

'I like my creature comforts,' said Max, and led her upstairs to look at the bedrooms. 'Well?'

'Wow!' Abby gazed in awe at the huge bed in the master bedroom.

'Don't worry, I shan't throw you on that and ravish you,' he said lightly.

'I know. I remember the deal. I have to throw *you* on it,' she said, smiling at him. 'I could hardly miss if I did. That could sleep four in a pinch.'

'But it's perfect just for two.' He took her hand to lead her from the room. 'Though not right now.'

Max took her up to the top of the house to show her the attic rooms he'd converted into a vast study to accommodate his antiquarian drawing board and the computers and high-tech tools of his profession.

Abby inspected it all, deeply impressed. 'If I weren't here would you be working on something today?'

'Probably.' He kissed her lightly. 'But I'm going to laze the day away with you instead.'

They put a simple cold lunch together and ate it in Max's

state-of-the-art kitchen, then shared one of his wonderfully comfortable sofas to read the Sunday papers. Abby felt her eyes drooping as she read through the book reviews, and woke with a start to find she'd fallen asleep on Max's shoulder.

'Sorry, Max. Some kind of lunch guest I turned out to be!'

He kissed her briefly. 'Don't worry. You snore very prettily.'

'I do not snore!'

'How do you know?'

Abby laughed. 'I don't, of course. Do you?'

'I've never had any complaints,' he said smugly, and pulled her to her feet to lead her to the kitchen.

She eyed him narrowly. 'I'd forgotten that you've had a serious relationship. '

'Does it bother you?' he asked, filling a kettle.

She nodded. 'It does a bit. When we're together you'll have comparisons to make. I won't.'

Max pulled out a chair for her at the table. 'I promise there'll be no comparisons. The relationship ended painlessly a long time ago.'

'She didn't live here, then?' said Abby, relieved.

'No.' He turned away to make tea. 'Since the move I've been too busy getting the firm up and running for much time for a social life. I attend the events that help raise the firm's profile, of course. Useful contacts are the name of the game. And my partners' wives invite me round to supper regularly, usually to pair me off with some unattached friend. Just like your problem with Rachel.' Max handed her a tall porcelain mug of tea. 'I pay them back in restaurants, but you can preside over my first dinner party here soon and show them I'm well and truly spoken for.'

Abby eyed him in alarm. 'You're not serious!'

'I am, but don't panic. I have something else in mind for you first.' Max sat down beside her. 'You're not working right now, and I had to cut short my stay in Italy recently, so how do you feel about spending a long weekend with me in Todi while the weather's still good? Aldo Zanini wants me to approve some old paving stones he's salvaged for the courtyard at the back of the house.'

Abby stared at him, her mind working overtime. 'It's a tempting idea,' she said cautiously.

'You could explore Todi to your heart's content—and you could have your own room,' added Max, cutting straight to the heart of her qualms. 'Other than my father and Gianni, and Aldo and his crew, of course, no one really appreciates what's been achieved at the house. You've had a fleeting glimpse of it, but I want you to see it all, so will you come?'

'Of course I will,' she said without hesitation. 'Once I start work again I won't have time for a while. I'd love to come.'

For the rest of the week Max rang every evening, but Abby saw no more of him until very early the following Friday, when he picked her up to drive to the airport. She had been watching impatiently for the car, and the moment it stopped at the gate she flew out of the house and down the path, straight into his outstretched arms.

'God, it's been a long week,' he said, between kisses. 'But to take off with a clear conscience I had to work like the devil, which meant no distractions. Have you missed me?'

'Yes,' she said tersely, which was the truth. Abby had kept busy with job applications, housework and making meals for her mother, who was now back at school, and Rachel had come round one evening, full of wedding plans. But for someone used to a hectic London lifestyle the time had dragged otherwise for Abby. Isabel had a long-established social life of her own, and because Abby wouldn't hear of her mother staying in on her account every night, the main highlight of most days had been the nightly telephone conversation with Max. 'I must find something to do soon,' she said, as he stowed her bags in the car. 'I'm not cut out to be a lady of leisure.'

Max shot her a searching look as they set off. 'Is the financial angle worrying you?'

'No. At least not yet. As I told you, Simon was very generous. I need occupation, not money.'

'What have you tried for so far?'

'A job with one of the executives of an investment bank and another in human resources in a distribution company. Not really my cup of tea, either of them, but I suppose I was spoilt because my first job dropped into my lap and I enjoyed it so much. Not to worry,' she added philosophically. 'Something will turn up.'

Travelling with Max was a very pleasant experience. The day was sunny for the drive to the airport, their flight left on time, and after landing in Florence they caught a train to Perugia to pick up the car Max had hired in advance.

'Are you tired?' he asked as he drove off.

'A bit. But pleasantly so.' Abby smiled at him 'I'm hungry, though.'

'We'll stop in Todi for supplies. Or we can have dinner there.'

'Not tonight. Let's buy lots of bread and cheese and tomatoes and have a picnic in front of that great fireplace of yours.'

'Sounds good to me.' Max put out a hand to touch her knee. 'Given sufficient persuasion, I might even light a fire for you.'

Abby looked at him in surprise. 'Will it be cold enough for that?'

'It can get chilly on my hilltop.'

'Have you told Gianni we're coming?'

Max shook his head. 'I want you all to myself this weekend. We can see him another time.'

By the time they'd done some shopping in Todi and set off again for Max's house, Abby was beginning to yawn. The journey was longer via the less terrifying route, and it was dark when the car began to climb up, ascending curves that were more forgiving than the tight hairpin bends of the other road, but still challenging enough for Abby to respect anyone who cycled to Max's house that way.

'We've arrived,' he announced as the car nosed into the unpaved courtyard at the back of the house. He switched off the ignition and leaned over to kiss her. 'Welcome back to my retreat, or Il Rifugio, as Gianni calls it.'

Abby took charge of the groceries as Max carried their luggage into a large kitchen with a stone fireplace similar to the one she remembered in the living room. A central island separated the eating space from a cooking area with gleaming modern appliances, yet the room still managed to retain the feel of the farmhouse that had originally stood on the property.

'This is such a fabulous kitchen,' she said, delighted.

'I'm glad you like it. But I'll take you up to your room before we start thinking about food.' He relieved her of the groceries and led her out into the hall. 'I sleep on the top floor; you can have one of the guest rooms on the one below. But don't spend too long in your bathroom. I'm hungry!'

'Just a wash and brush up and I'll be with you,' she assured him as they went up the shallow stairs.

Max led her to a door at the far end of the landing but stopped dead so suddenly when he opened it that Abby bumped into him, her eyes like saucers as she peered over his shoulder. The room was charming, with a beamed ceiling and tester bed with gauzy white hangings which revealed two naked entwined bodies only partially covered by a white quilt.

CHAPTER EIGHT

MAX BACKED away very quietly, touching a finger to his lips as he took Abby by the hand. He led her downstairs to the living room and closed the door behind them.

'You obviously know Gianni's mystery lady,' said Abby, bursting with curiosity. 'So don't just stand there, laughing. Who is she?'

'Renata!'

Abby stared at him. 'Your cleaner? But she's so *young*. I pictured someone like Rosa!'

'You're not far out. When I asked Rosa to recommend someone to look after my house, she said the utterly trustworthy niece who helped her out at Villa Falcone sometimes would be very glad of the money. Renata's a music student and needs the extra cash.'

'Music? Does she sing too?'

'No—at least not as far as I know. Renata's studying piano.'

Abby's eyes danced. 'Better still. She can accompany Gianni, help him rehearse and so on.'

'By the look of what we saw upstairs it's the "so on" he likes most!' Max sobered abruptly as he remembered his mother. 'Oh, my God—I can just imagine what Luisa will say when she finds out.'

Abby frowned. 'Because the love of Gianni's life is Rosa's niece?'

'Absolutely. Luisa will want him to marry someone far more exalted than Renata Berni—' Max stood up as Gianni burst into the room, hair dishevelled and his eyes imploring as he let loose a torrent of Italian on his brother before checking in surprise when he saw Abby.

'Forgive me, I did not know…' He thrust a hand through his hair, colour flooding his handsome face. 'You saw us, Abby?'

'She most certainly did,' said Max blandly. 'I was just showing Abby where to sleep, but the bed was occupied.'

Gianni coloured even more deeply and gave Max a straight look. 'I will give you back your key if you wish.'

'Of course I don't. You keep it. Renata has one of her own, anyway. Where is she?'

'She is putting fresh sheets on the bed to avoid facing you,' said Gianni despondently. 'She is not only embarrassed, she is worried that you will not let her work for you any more.'

'She has far more to worry about than that—our lady mother for one,' said Max dryly. 'But tell her not to worry on my account; her job is safe.'

'Why not bring her down?' suggested Abby soothingly. 'I'd like to meet her.'

Gianni brightened and kissed her on both cheeks. '*Grazie*. I will fetch her.'

Max shook his head in wonder as they heard Gianni racing up the stairs. 'I can't believe this. He's known Renata all her life. Her mother—Rosa's sister—died when she was young so Zia Rosa has been bringing her to the villa since she was small.'

'Is she pretty?'

Max thought about it. 'Not so long ago she was a skinny little kid with her hair in braids, but these days "pretty" isn't exactly the word for Renata.'

When Gianni led the girl into the room a moment later

Abby saw what Max meant. Even in her desperate, tear-stained embarrassment, Renata Berni was breathtaking. Tumbled, curling hair framed a face with huge dark eyes, chiselled cheekbones and a mouth like a ripe peach.

Gianni put his arm round her protectively and drew her close. 'Do not be angry, Max.'

'Of course I'm not angry,' said Max impatiently, and turned to the girl with a reassuring smile. 'I will speak English today, Renata, so listen carefully. I'm definitely not angry. You can keep your job here for as long as you want. Now, let me introduce Miss Abigail Green, the lady I'm going to marry.'

The girl relaxed as Max spoke, and at last managed a shy smile for Abby. *'Piacere,'* she said, in a low, husky voice as sexy as her mouth. 'I am so happy for you.'

'Thank you, Renata,' said Abby warmly. 'Max tells me you're a pianist.'

'A student only,' she demurred, and gave Gianni an adoring look. 'But I play good enough to help Gianni.'

'Renata is very talented. She accompanies me sometimes when I rehearse,' he said proudly, then took in a deep breath, stood very erect and drew the girl closer. 'We love each other, you understand.'

'Oh, yes,' said his brother dryly. 'We understand. But Luisa won't.'

Renata blenched at the name and shrank closer to her lover. 'Signor Max, will you tell her?'

'No. Gianni must do that.' Max grinned. 'And at least you're not married, Renata, which was my main worry.'

'Ah, but she *is* married,' said Gianni, and spoke to the girl in rapid Italian. She looked up at him uncertainly, but he smiled and nodded lovingly, and at last she drew a gold chain from her T-shirt.

Max and Abby stared in silence at the plain gold ring hanging from it.

'Renata is now my wife,' said Gianni proudly.

'Is she, by God? When did this happen?' demanded Max.

'Since I am becoming well known her father would not let her see me any more, so I said we must marry.'

'But why did he object?' said Abby, astonished.

'He thinks now Gianni is big celebrity he will take me as lover then leave me,' said Renata unhappily.

'But surely he would have felt differently if Gianni had asked to marry you?' said Max.

'My father is old. Also he has bad heart,' said Renata, shivering. 'I beg Gianni to wait.'

'But I could not wait,' said Gianni huskily and caught her close. 'So I persuade her to marry me in secret. *Allora*, in a little while we tell Mamma, and then Renata's father has no choice. He must accept me as her husband.' He shot an apologetic look at his brother. 'Until then we meet here in secret when I am home, where no one can see us.'

'I don't mind.' Max shook his head. 'But you were risking it.'

Gianni threw out his hands. 'It is natural that I check on my brother's house, no? And it is known that Renata comes here to clean for you. Though I do not like this. Now she is my wife she has no need to work—'

'But I must have a job,' broke in Renata urgently, 'so my father knows where I get money.'

Max frowned. 'But you only come here twice a week. It can't be enough for you!'

'It is not,' said Gianni with a smouldering look at his bride. 'We come often when I am home. Renata hides her bicycle inside the woodshed when she should not be here.'

Max shook his head. 'You can hardly hide the Lamborghini.'

'I borrow Rosa's car,' said Gianni simply.

'Ah. Rosa's in on the secret, then!'

Renata nodded shyly. 'Zia Rosa came to the wedding. She tell my father she need my help with driving to Perugia.'

'And they do drive to Perugia,' added Gianni. 'But I meet them there, and we go on to Ravenna where Rosa knows a priest. She arranged everything.'

'Of course she did,' said Max dryly. 'So when are you going to let Luisa in on the secret?'

Gianni squared his shoulders. 'For a while I have many engagements, also much time in the recording studio. So I shall tell Mamma when she comes to spend Christmas at the Villa Falcone.' He gave Max a sly smile. 'You would like to join us, no?'

'No! If I did Luisa would find some way to blame me for the whole thing,' retorted Max. He turned to Renata with a warm smile and embraced her. 'Welcome to the family, *cara*. Gianni is a lucky man.'

Abby added her good wishes as she bent to kiss the girl. 'Bring your beautiful bride to London, Gianni, when you come for the concert.'

'I will,' he promised, and smiled at her gratefully. 'Max is also a lucky man. And he owes me, no?' he said, wagging a finger at his brother. 'Do not forget—I brought you two together!'

There was an impassioned argument as the happy pair prepared to leave, most of which was lost on Abby as Gianni insisted and Renata vehemently shook her head.

'She's right, Gianni,' said Max, intervening. 'If you want to keep your secret you can't drive Renata down to the village. I will. Help me put her bike in the car, and then you take off in the other direction.'

While Max was out Abby put their simple supper together, and looked up expectantly when he came in. 'Juliet safely delivered?'

He grinned. 'Yes. Did you manage to send Romeo on his way?'

'Not without difficulty. He wanted to talk. In the end I said

I was tired and wanted a bath, so he kissed me and took off down that road like a rocket.' She shook her head. 'If he's not careful Renata will be a widow before she's a proper wife.'

'At least he wasn't in the Lamborghini. Did you have your bath?'

'No. I didn't fancy it on my own in the house. But I'd like one before we eat, please.'

'Right. While you're doing that I'll light the fire.' Max kissed her swiftly. 'Sorry I was so long.'

'Don't worry, I wasn't bored.' She chuckled. 'My visits to this part of the world tend to be amazingly eventful so far!'

'The scene in my guest room was certainly a surprise,' Max admitted, laughing.

Abby smiled fondly. 'They looked so beautiful lying there in each other's arms, like a sculpture by Canova. Is Gianni's agent in on the secret?'

'I shouldn't think so. Why?'

'If he was he'd surely want to cash in on the publicity. A more gorgeous pair than our Romeo and Juliet would be hard to find. Just imagine the photographs!'

'Bath,' said Max firmly, and caught her by the hand to march her to the door. 'Forget about Gianni and Renata for a while. I'm hungry.'

In the guest room, which Renata had left as immaculate as though no one had set foot in it, Abby unpacked swiftly, then showered and dressed at top speed and went back down to Max in jeans and the heavy crimson sweater she'd thought she wouldn't need.

'You were right,' she said, as she went into the living room. 'It does get chilly up here. That fire looks wonderful.'

'So do you,' said Max, adding another log to the blaze. 'Sit here. I'll fetch the food.'

'We'll do that together,' she said, and smiled up at him. 'I really love it here, Max.'

He put an arm round her as they crossed the hall to the kitchen. 'In that case, *fidanzata mia*, we'll come here for our honeymoon.'

Instead of panic at the mere idea, Abby felt a warm thrill of anticipation as she reached up to press her lips to Max's cheek. 'Good idea,' she said happily, and piled olives, tomatoes, cheese, and slivers of San Daniele ham on big white plates. Max put them on a tray with a basket of bread and Abby carried the wine into the main room. She gave a sigh of pure satisfaction as they settled on the sofa to eat the meal by the light of flames flickering on earth-toned walls.

'I was starving,' said Max, as he put a slice of pecorino on a hunk of bread.

'Me too.' Abby did the same and added a slice of ham. 'But tomorrow we must buy food I can cook.'

'We could go down to Todi to eat,' he suggested, mouth full.

'Only to shop and have a look round again. I'd rather eat here on our own—what is it?' she added, when she saw him gazing at her with a strange look in his eye.

He smiled slowly. 'It suddenly struck me that not so long ago I didn't know you existed. Gianni's right. I should be grateful to him. Without him we would never have met.'

Abby nodded. 'We owe him a good turn. Maybe we should lend our support when he confesses to your mother.'

'You're willing to do that?' he said, impressed.

'If it would help, yes. Though I suppose you'd have to introduce me to her first.' Abby frowned as she nibbled on a piece of cheese. 'But I'm no more exalted than Renata. She'll probably object to me, too.'

'Luisa is unlikely to care who *I* marry.' Max's mouth twisted. 'Nor would I take any notice if she did.'

Abby sighed as she put her empty plate on the sturdy table in front of the sofa. 'It's such a pity, Max.'

'What is?'

'Your relationship with your mother. From that photograph of you together when you were small, she obviously doted on you.'

'Not enough to make her stay with me.'

'Your father said she pleaded to take you with her, remember.'

'True.' Max got up to put another log on the fire. 'I wonder how things would have turned out if she had.'

'Not much differently, because your father wouldn't have let her keep you there.' Abby regarded his broad shoulders thoughtfully. 'I'd like to meet your mother, Max. Once, anyway.'

He turned, smiling crookedly. 'Once will be enough if the meeting coincides with Gianni's grand confession.'

'But if his mother refuses to welcome Renata as his wife she risks alienating him completely—and surely she loves him too much to want that.'

'To understand Luisa's point of view you need to know her background.' Max piled dishes on the tray. 'I'll just sort these out, then I'll tell you a story.'

Abby got up quickly and held the door open for him. 'We'll do it together.'

Max strode into the kitchen, dumped the tray on the table and took her in his arms. 'I love you, Abby,' he whispered, and kissed her hard. 'And just for the record, I've never said that to a woman before.'

'Good,' she said succinctly. 'Make sure you don't say it to anyone else in future, either. I'm the jealous type. How about you?'

His arms tightened. 'You probably guessed that the day I met Marcus Kent.'

Abby detached herself and began loading the dishwasher. 'You have absolutely no need to be jealous of Marcus,' she assured him. 'So, come on, I want to hear this story.'

When they went back to the living room Max put another log on the fire before joining Abby on the sofa.

'Hurry up,' she said peremptorily. 'I'm expiring with curiosity here.'

He chuckled. 'All right, all right. Once upon a time, then, in a little village a few miles from Todi, Luisa Scotto surprised her parents by arriving long after they'd given up all hope of having children. Papa was a farm hand, so in their household money was tight, with respectability second only to God. After school little Luisa, the child of her parents' old age, helped her mother cook and clean, but she yearned to go to college, and learn to be a teacher.'

'Her parents weren't keen on the idea?'

'No. They wanted her to marry some local boy, live at home and give them grandchildren.'

'Ah. Bad news for Luisa. So what happened?'

'She fell in love with the wrong local boy, a handsome tearaway by the name of Enzo Falcone. Determined to put his ewe lamb out of Enzo's reach, my grandfather ignored his wife's entreaties and packed Luisa off to London to work in his brother's café, just round the corner from the school where my father taught French and Italian. Enzo disappeared off the radar for a while, and the rest you know.'

'Fascinating,' said Abby. 'But you've obviously told me this for a reason.'

Max nodded. 'Luisa loved her parents, but not their poverty. Renata comes from much the same type of background. Not at all what Mamma wants for her Gianni.'

Abby stared into the flames thoughtfully. 'When your mother met up with Enzo again he'd obviously made his fortune. Would she have gone back to him if he was still poor?'

'Definitely. She loved him with a passion he returned in full. When he died suddenly the light went out of Luisa's life. Gianni is her great consolation—a pretty heavy burden for the lad, and one he shoulders with very good grace.' Max shrugged. 'But, now he's married, his mother will just have to knuckle down and accept Renata as his wife.'

'Renata's father will have to knuckle down too.'

'True. Though an alliance with Luisa Scotto won't be something Papa Berni relishes.'

'Why not?'

'When Luisa met Enzo again she became pregnant with Gianni right away, but it was a long time before she and Enzo could actually marry.' Max shrugged. 'While Enzo was alive she didn't care about the wagging tongues, but without him she prefers to live in Venice, where no one knows her past.'

'It's not so very terrible a past, Max!'

'It is to someone brought up like Luisa. Everyone in the village knew that the father of her second child was her old lover, not her English husband—bad news for my Scotto grandparents.'

'Do you ever visit them?'

'Yes, but they died when I was in my teens. Luisa pleaded their age as her reason for coming back so often, but I think she was desperate to look for Enzo as much as to visit them.' Max gazed into the fire. 'When Luisa was sent away Enzo took off on his old Ducati and travelled all over Italy, doing whatever work he could find. Then he had a stroke of luck, won a huge sum of money in a lottery, and instead of spending it as fast as he could he made shrewd investments in property.'

'Didn't he try to get in touch with Luisa?'

'She was married by then. Enzo told me when I was older that he was heartbroken when he heard, and tried to forget her.'

Abby looked up into Max's face. 'But he stayed single?'

He shrugged. 'A man with Enzo's looks must have had women throwing themselves at him, but he certainly never married until he met Luisa again.'

'It's a very romantic story, Max.'

'I suppose it is.'

She chuckled. 'You don't sound very enthusiastic.'

Max lifted her onto this lap, kissed her briefly and held her close. 'I'm more enthusiastic about *our* story, Abigail Green.'

Abby relaxed against him, feeling drowsy in the warmth from the flames. 'I am, too,' she said sleepily.

'You're tired,' he said softly. 'Do you want to go to bed?'

'Not yet. I want to stay just like this for a while,' she said, yawning. 'You know, Max, it's hard to believe that since I first saw this room life has changed so much for us.'

Max rubbed a cheek over her hair. 'When the house was finished I couldn't put my finger on what was missing. Then I met you and the last piece of the puzzle fell into place.'

She reached up to kiss him. 'Tomorrow,' she said, settling back comfortably, 'I want to see the view from every single window in the house.'

'You can do whatever you want,' he promised, and laughed as a yawn overwhelmed her again. 'But, right now, it's time you were in bed.'

Max set her on her feet, then took her by the hand to walk up the stairs to the room that had been so startlingly occupied earlier on. 'All yours now,' he said, opening the door. 'Goodnight, darling. Sleep well.'

Abby held up her face for his kiss, and put her arms round him, burrowing her face against his chest. 'I love you, Max Wingate.'

'I love you too,' he said in a constricted voice. He detached her arms and turned her round, sending her through the door with an unromantic tap on her behind. 'Off you go, Abigail,' he said sternly, and closed the door on her.

Abby woke next morning to the heavenly scent of fresh coffee, and blinked sleepily as she saw Max smiling down at her, steaming mug in hand.

'Good morning, darling. Or *buon giorno*, as we say in these parts. Sit up. Did you sleep?'

'I certainly did. Good morning to you, too.' Abby struggled up, yawning, to let Max prop pillows behind her.

'Is that the kind of thing you sleep in?' he asked, eyeing her thick rugby shirt.

'No. But I was cold last night.' She smiled at him. 'I almost came to share your bed.'

'I wouldn't have turned you away,' he assured her. 'I'm not a saint, Abigail.'

'Good!' Abby downed her coffee and handed him the mug. 'Give me five minutes and I'll be with you.'

Max had heated yesterday's rolls and had orange juice and more coffee ready by the time Abby got downstairs. But she jumped up to clear away the moment they'd finished breakfast, impatient to start on her tour of the house.

'The sun is shining and I can't wait to look at the views!' she said firmly. 'I've seen the one from the guest room, but you said the view from your bedroom was the best.'

The blocks of cypress laid on the upper floor gave the entire house the individual scent Abby had been too tired to identify the night before. She sniffed ecstatically and Max followed her, smiling, as she darted from one window to another to look out at the particular section of view each one framed. When they came to the master bedroom on the top floor, Abby gave only a cursory look at the abstract painting on the wall over the bed before hurrying out onto a small covered terrace to gaze down at the sunlit panorama below.

'Wow! You were right. This is the best view of all.' She leaned out over the stone parapet in excitement. 'I can see the pool from here.'

'Aldo lined the old threshing ground with concrete he painted grey to make it look like a natural pond. It should be warm enough to sit out there later, if you like.' Max put an arm round her as they leaned against the parapet together. 'So, now you've thoroughly inspected it, do you like my house?'

'How could I not?' She rubbed her cheek against his sleeve thoughtfully. 'But it must have cost a fortune to restore. Do you let it out to tourists to make it pay?'

'No. When Enzo left me the property, he also left me enough money to maintain the house as well as rebuild it, so I don't have to rent it out. My father comes here with me sometimes, and of course your family is welcome to make use of it. But otherwise it's strictly private.'

'Which leaves Gianni and Renata free to use it as a love-nest,' said Abby, smiling.

'If Luisa finds that out there'll be hell to pay,' he said grimly. 'Come on, let's go shopping.'

As they approached it later, the walls of Todi rose up before them, like a Renaissance painting in the morning sunlight.

'On one of my visits here this place was full of Hell's Angels,' said Max, when they reached the Piazza del Populo. 'It was quite a sight to see them all streaming away on their bikes, with a police car in front and an ambulance bringing up the rear.'

'Unexpected in a town like Todi,' agreed Abby, finding the scene hard to imagine against the romantic medieval backdrop.

'Look, let's have an early lunch here and take home something easy to eat tonight,' said Max. 'I haven't brought you here to slave over a stove.'

'Done.' She grinned at him. 'Would it offend your aesthetic sensibilities if I asked for pizza?'

'You can have anything you want. But we buy the food for supper before we eat. Shops close for lunch in these parts.'

It was late in the afternoon when they got back to the house, and Abby made only a half-hearted protest when Max suggested she had a rest on her bed.

'It must be this glorious air you have up here—it knocks

me out. But what are you going to do?' she asked as they went into the kitchen.

'I thought I'd go down to Aldo's yard and take a look at these paving stones he's found—hello!' He dumped down the grocery bags as he saw the dishes on the island. One contained meatballs in a rich tomato sauce, the other *strangozzi*, the local pasta. Max smiled as he read the note that lay on top. 'Renata hopes this will be acceptable for our dinner, and apologises for embarrassing us yesterday.'

Abby shook her head in wonder as she inspected the meatballs. 'That girl's such a star! She's a raving beauty, a talented pianist and a fabulous cook into the bargain. No wonder Gianni snapped her up so quickly.'

Max kissed Abby goodbye, eyeing her doubtfully. 'I'm not keen on leaving you here alone. Are you sure you won't come with me?'

'Yes. I've brought a couple of books so I'll have a read while you're out. But don't be too long.' She smiled up at him. 'See you later.'

Abby went up to her room and stood at the window for a while to look at her section of the view. Sunlight poured like molten gold over the hills and vineyards, and for the first time she could make out the battlements of some ancient building in the far distance. She stood, just gazing for a while, and then settled down in the picturesque bed to read. Later she got up to have a shower, pulled on her gold velvet trousers and clinging black sweater, and decided a lipstick was the only touch needed for a face glowing very satisfactorily after wandering round Todi in the autumn sunlight. As she brushed her hair loose on her shoulders, her eyes lit up at the sound of someone downstairs. Max was back. She left the bedroom and ran barefoot along the landing, then stopped dead as she reached the head of the stairs. An elegantly dressed young woman with gleaming dark hair stood in the hall below, peering into the living room. As she heard Abby's intake of breath she turned, and glared up at her with dark, deep-set eyes that were all too familiar.

CHAPTER NINE

LUISA FALCONE beckoned Abby down the stairs with an imperious gesture, speaking in a torrent of Italian too swift and impassioned for Abby to understand other than that it was hostile. Wishing she had shoes on, Abby went down reluctantly, praying that Max would come back soon. But until he did she had to keep cool. Whatever his feelings towards her, this woman was his mother, who at close quarters looked nearer the age she must actually be.

'I'm sorry, I don't understand,' Abby said, when she could edge a word in. 'I don't speak Italian.' The effect was dramatic. Cut off in mid-flow, Luisa stared at her blankly.

'Perche no?' she said incredulously.

'I'm British. My name is Abigail Green.'

Luisa eyed her in frowning incomprehension. 'It is *you* who are here with my son?'

'Yes. He went out for while, but he'll be back soon.'

'Non importa!' Luisa shrugged impatiently. 'It is you I came to see. This stops now, you understand? I forbid you to meet my son in secret here, whoever you are. I will not allow you to ruin his life.' The dark eyes narrowed ominously. 'If it is money you want I will pay—'

'That's enough!' ordered a peremptory voice, and Abby

turned in relief as Max emerged from the kitchen. 'You've made a very embarrassing mistake, Mother.'

Luisa spun round, eyes wide. *'Massimo?* What are you doing here?'

'It *is* my house,' he drawled. 'More to the point, what are *you* doing here? You can hardly say you were passing.' Two pairs of identical eyes met and clashed, Luisa's the first to fall.

'I made Rosa give me her key,' she said, her accent more pronounced as colour rose in her beautiful face. 'I came by taxi from the train in Perugia, as a surprise for Gianni, but he was not at the villa. Rosa pretended she did not know where he was. I thought he must be here at your house with this—this woman of his, so I took a local taxi here to confront her.' She looked at Abby. 'I apologise for the mistake,' she said stiffly.

'Not at all,' said Abby politely. 'Shall we sit somewhere comfortable? Would you like coffee, or a glass of wine?'

Luisa hesitated, took a look at her son's face and shook her head. 'Thank you, but no. I must not stay.'

'Why did you think Gianni would be here?' asked Max.

She shrugged. 'I know he comes up here to your house sometimes. I am sure he meets his woman here.' She touched her breast. 'I feel it in my heart. But this must stop, Max. I will not let him to ruin his career.'

'Gianni's twenty-five, financially independent, and his career is doing very nicely,' Max pointed out. 'Face it, Mother. He can live his life any way he chooses.'

'Of course your support is for him always. Not for me,' said his mother bitterly. 'Yet I only want what is best for him.'

'Or what *you* think is best for him.' Max took Abby's hand. 'If you can stop thinking of Gianni for a minute, perhaps you would like a formal introduction. Allow me to present Miss Abigail Green, my *fidanzata.*'

Luisa's slanting eyebrows rose in surprise. She seemed lost for words for a moment. *'Piacere,'* she said at last, and forced a smile. 'I regret that our first meeting is so unfortunate. I did not know you were here, of course. Max does not inform me of his arrangements.'

'I'm very glad to meet you, Signora Falcone,' said Abby, and smiled coaxingly. 'Won't you have that wine now?'

Luisa glanced at Max again, then shook her head. 'Thank you, no. I must get back to the Villa Falcone. If I may use your telephone, Max, to call a taxi?' she said with formality.

'No need. I'll drive you down.'

'*Grazie.*' Luisa turned to Abby. 'I hope we meet again soon.'

'Thank you. I'll look forward to that.'

Max took Abby in his arms and kissed her. 'I won't be long, darling.'

Abby waited in the open doorway, waving goodbye as Max helped his mother into the car. So that was the famous, beautiful Luisa. Max was right. She looked nowhere near old enough to be his mother. Abby shuddered. Thank heavens Luisa hadn't turned up yesterday and caught the lovers in bed. Young Renata was no match for her mother-in-law. It would be a pity, all the same, if Luisa Falcone refused to accept her as Gianni's wife. She could end up alienated from both her sons.

Abby went upstairs for shoes and a book, then laid the kitchen table for dinner, but decided against putting the meatballs to heat in case Max wanted a shower before he ate. Wishing she'd thought to bring some tea bags, she drank mineral water in preference to coffee, then went round the house turning on lights. At last she curled up on the sofa in the living room with her book and settled down to wait.

At first she managed to concentrate on the story, but as the minutes dragged past she grew so worried she was frantic by the time she finally heard the car drive into the courtyard. She ran to open the front door, her heart plummeting as she saw Max's drawn, haggard face.

'Darling, what is it? Do you feel ill?' she demanded.

'No.' He smiled so bleakly her heart contracted. 'I'm sorry I left you alone so long, but would you mind if dinner waited a while, Abby? I need a bath and a few minutes to relax. Don't worry,' he added, as they went into the house. 'I often need time to recover after an encounter with Luisa.'

'Take as long as you like,' she said with sympathy. 'When you come down you can have a leisurely drink while I deal with Renata's dinner.'

Max touched a hand to her cheek, then walked wearily upstairs. Abby gazed after him for a moment, then went into the sitting room again to read, but after half an hour she decided it was time to hurry him up. Abby went quietly up to his room and found it in darkness when she put her head round the door. She could just make out the dark shape of Max's body, lying prone on the white cover, his face buried in his crossed arms.

Abby tiptoed over to the bed, her eyes suddenly wide in consternation when she realised that his shoulders were moving slightly. Max was crying.

She sat on the bed beside him and stroked his thick damp hair. She waited, tense, for him to shrug her hand away, but he lay utterly still under her caress, and, taking courage, she lay down beside him and pulled his head to her breast and held him close, murmuring formless words of comfort. For a while he lay utterly quiet, his tears seeping hot through the thin wool of her sweater, but at last his arms closed round her like bands of steel, and Abby kissed his hair and his forehead and put a gentle finger under his chin to raise his face to hers. She felt a great shudder run through him as their lips met, and he began kissing her with a frantic, desperate hunger she responded to in kind, fierce in her need to comfort. His hands moved over her body, setting her on fire as he moulded her against him. His hands probed beneath her sweater, hot on her bare skin, and suddenly, urgently, he was undressing her and she was helping him until at last she was naked in his arms.

Max groaned like a man in pain at the touch of her body against his, but she held him close, licking the tears from the corners of his eyes as she ran her hands down his naked back. His mouth travelled down her throat to kiss the lovely curve between neck and shoulder, then on to the taut tips of her breasts, and she felt a thrill run through her down to her toes as his lips pulled gently on her nipples. When she felt the graze of his teeth, she sucked in a deep breath and thrust her hips against his erection. Breathing harshly, he turned her on her back and hung over her, his eyes wild in the gloom as they questioned hers. Abby answered by reaching up to bring his mouth down on hers, her body trembling in anticipation as his caressing fingers moved up her thighs, then he waited motionless until her fingernails beat an urgent tattoo on his shoulders. She gave a little choking sound as the skilled fingers roused sensations which arched her body against him in clamouring response that obliterated any trace of panic.

'Now,' she said gruffly, in a voice she hardly recognised as her own, and Max kissed her in triumphant possession as he entered her. She tilted her hips to accept the hard, rigid length of him, but Max was gentle, entering her slowly, little by little, until at last he was deep inside her and she discovered for the first time what it really meant to be one flesh. Then conscious thought stopped as he began to move, and Abby gasped and moved with him, her body hesitant at first, then bolder, soon reaching such accord with his they surged together in a seductive, relentless rhythm that speeded them at last to the climax she experienced first, and Max held her close until his own release engulfed him and he collapsed on her, his face buried against her breasts.

After a long, silent interval Max turned on his back and

held her close in the crook of his arm, his breathing still ragged as he fought to adjust to the dizzying ascent from despair to the heights of rapture.

'Why were you crying?' asked Abby at last.

Max smoothed a hand over her hair. 'My darling, I can't talk about that yet. I will, soon, but right now I just want to lie here with you in my arms for a while to convince myself that I'm not dreaming.'

'If you are I shared the dream—in every way possible!'

'No panic at all?'

Abby thought about it. 'A bit. But only when I thought you might get where we were going before I did.' She felt him shake with laughter and relaxed. 'Funny to think I used to wonder if I'd know when I had an orgasm—in the unlikely event that I ever had one, of course.'

'The same way you'd know if you fell over a cliff! Speaking from my own viewpoint.'

'Mine too. I was absolutely astounded. Does it happen every time?'

'It does for me. And if you care to repeat the experience I'll do my best to make sure it does for you, too.' Max pulled her close and pressed kisses all over her face.

Abby sighed blissfully. 'I've been such an idiot. I'm sorry, Max.'

'Why?'

'For the stupid panic before. I never thought of that tonight. I just knew you needed me.'

'God, yes,' he said thickly, and kissed her hard. 'And in the end your pity overcame the panic.'

Abby gave him a shove. 'Did it feel like pity?'

'No.' He reached out to switch on a bedside lamp and looked into her eyes. 'It felt like I'd died and gone to heaven.'

She smiled, swallowing a lump in her throat at the sight of his swollen eyelids. 'I did, too, so that's all right, then.' She bit her lip as her stomach gave a sudden, noisy rumble. 'Gosh, how unromantic.'

Max laughed and scooped her up to carry her into the bathroom. 'We'll have a shower, then go down and eat. Thank God for Renata and her *polpette di carne.*'

Showering together was another new experience for Abby, and a lot of fun, she discovered; so much fun that it would have led them straight back to bed if they hadn't been so hungry.

'Odd,' she said, as she dressed afterwards. 'I couldn't cope with sex at all before, but now I think I could easily get addicted to it.'

Max shook his head as he tugged down his heavy sweater. 'Sex is for one-night stands. Making love is for lovers.'

'Is that what we are?'

He brushed a lock of hair back from her face and kissed her. 'Yes, my darling, that's exactly what we are.'

Abby made no more mention of Max's tears as she got busy with their dinner. If he explained at all he must do it in his own time. He gave her a glass of wine and sat down at the table, looking at ease with the world as he watched her.

'These smell wonderful,' she said, checking the temperature of the meatballs. 'Would you know what she puts in them?'

Max got up to inspect them. 'Pork ground up with onion and a little garlic,' he said, sniffing. 'The green bits are probably parsley, and there must be some dry breadcrumbs in there to hold it all together. I've seen Rosa frying them to seal the flavour before simmering them in the tomato sauce, so Renata probably learned from her.'

'What would anyone do without Rosa?' Abby drained the pasta and added it to the dish with the steaming meatballs, then ladled the mixture into the bowls Max carried to the table. He held her chair for her then sat opposite, smiling into her eyes.

'To us,' he said, raising his glass.

Abby echoed the toast, then both of them fell on the meal

so ravenously it was some time before either of them said another word.

'If making love has this effect on my appetite,' said Abby at one stage, mopping up sauce with bread, 'I'll put on weight!'

Max grinned lasciviously. 'No problem—just more of you to kiss.'

She shook her head in wonder. 'I still can't believe it finally happened, Max. I never thought it would.'

'I knew it would. Otherwise why would fate send you up my road instead of Gianni's?' Max put down his fork, looking at her steadily. 'But because it happened so suddenly, when I was totally off-guard, I didn't give a thought to protection.'

'Not a problem,' she assured him blithely. 'I did.' She shrugged as his eyes narrowed in surprise. 'Laura saw to that before I went up to Trinity.'

'Sensible lady!'

'Of course, until now it's never been necessary,' said Abby, and got up to take their bowls, eyeing her watch in surprise. 'I didn't realise it was so late.'

'I'll make you some coffee,' said Max, clearing the table.

'No, thanks. I'll just take some water to bed.'

'Which bed?' he asked bluntly.

'Yours,' she said without hesitation, then bit her lip. 'If you want me to sleep there.'

Max threw back his head and laughed, then seized her in his arms, planting kisses all over her face. 'What kind of stupid question is that, Miss Clever?'

'The kind that needs an answer,' she said tartly.

Max leaned his forehead against hers. 'I've wanted you in my bed from the moment we met. Though preferably not in that rugby shirt you had on last night,' he added, thinking it over.

'Love me, love my shirt,' she retorted.

'Always!' He took a bottle from the refrigerator. 'Here's your water. Let's go to bed.'

They went upstairs hand in hand, but when they reached Abby's door she told him to go on up to his room. 'I'll join you in a few minutes.'

'Be quick,' he ordered, and planted a swift, hard kiss on her mouth as he gently pushed her inside.

Abby got through her usual night-time routine in such record time, Max was still in his bathroom brushing his teeth when she got to his bedroom. She hesitated, then took off her dressing gown and slid into the bed to wait for him, the covers pulled up to her chin.

Max turned off the taps and stood silhouetted in the bathroom doorway in a towelling robe. He looked at his watch, then switched off the bathroom light and made for the door to the landing.

'I'm here,' said Abby huskily, and he spun round, smiling, a look of such involuntary delight in his eyes her heart turned over.

'Well, well, look who's sleeping in my bed!'

'I'm not sleeping. Nor am I Goldilocks,' she said, rather less evenly than she'd intended.

'A raven-haired fairy princess, then,' he said, and sat down on the edge of the bed to curl a strand of gleaming hair round his finger. 'I was just going down to look for you. I thought you might have had second thoughts.'

'None at all. In fact, I rushed through all the girl night-time stuff to get back to you.' Abby smiled wryly. 'But it just struck me that I've never slept with anyone before, Max. I might be restless, keep you awake.'

'If you are I'll have to find some way to soothe you to sleep,' he said, eyes glinting, and touched the covers she'd drawn up to her chin. 'Are you cold?'

'No.'

'I suppose you're hiding that shirt from me,' he said, resigned.

'Are you going to talk all night or are you coming to bed?' she demanded.

Max chuckled and turned back the covers, then stood still. 'No shirt,' he said hoarsely.

'I thought you'd prefer me like this,' she whispered, and held up arms which were bare, like the rest of her.

Max shrugged off the dressing gown and instead of throwing himself on top of her, as every fibre of his body was urging him, he let himself down beside her and smoothed the long, slender curves of her body against his own. 'You are unbelievable, Abigail Green,' he said against her mouth. 'Have you any idea what it meant to me just then to find you here in my bed?'

'I hoped you'd be pleased,' she said in a stifled voice as his lips moved over her face.

'Pleased!' He took in a deep, shuddering breath. 'Pleased doesn't come near it. But,' he added, raising his head to look down at her, 'if you just want me to hold you like this and watch over you as you go to sleep, I'll do it. Somehow.'

'But you want to make love to me again.' She smiled. 'It's not something you can hide, is it?'

'No, you witch,' he said thickly as she thrust her hips against him. 'It's not. I was trying to be noble. But to hell with noble. I want you.'

'I want you, too,' she said breathlessly. 'And I never thought I'd say that to a man, ever.'

'Fate meant you to wait for me!' Max kissed her mouth and held her hands wide as his mouth moved down her throat and breasts, and past the slight swell of her belly. She stiffened as his mouth moved lower, and he released her hands to part her thighs to caress the most intimate, sensitive part of her. Abby gasped as she felt his hair brush against her moist, heated skin, and the lick of his tongue as it probed the inner secret folds until it reached a spot which brought her rearing up against him, helpless to control her reaction to the caresses which sent delicious waves of delicate sensation through her, and left her trembling afterwards while Max held her close and whispered gratifying things in her ear.

'Did you like that?' he asked, kissing her nose.

'I never imagined that I would, but I did.' She opened her eyes to look directly into his. 'Though I much prefer a duet to a solo.'

'I think that can be arranged—what is it?' he asked as her eyes widened.

'I can hardly believe I just said that.'

'Well, you did, so now you take the consequences,' Max warned, and entered her in one long, smooth thrust. He held her still, looking down into her eyes. 'Do you want me to stop?'

'No. I want you to move!' she said between her teeth, and he laughed exultantly and did as she demanded, keeping iron control over his own need as he dictated the pace to bring her slowly and relentlessly towards the goal Abby wanted to reach so fiercely that at last she dug her nails into his back and urged him into a speed she matched with such abandon they lay gasping in each other's arms afterwards awed by the passionate intensity of their mating.

It was much later when Abby realised that, deliciously comfortable though she might be, held close in Max's arms, she had no hope of getting any sleep while her question remained unanswered.

'Max?' she said quietly.

He drew her closer. 'What is it, my darling?'

'Why were you crying?'

CHAPTER TEN

MAX lay perfectly still, only the slight tightening of his arms indicating that he'd even heard the question.

'You don't have to tell me if it hurts too much,' Abby said quickly.

He shook his head. 'I want you to know. But it was too new and raw to put into words when I first got back.'

Abby looked up at the strong profile, clearly visible in the moonlit room. 'You had a quarrel with your mother on the way to the villa?'

'No. We survived the journey surprisingly well. The trouble kicked off when we arrived. Gianni was waiting for her, Luisa rushed to embrace him, and then made the worst mistake of her life.'

Luisa Falcone had burst into passionate tears as she forbade her beloved son to throw himself away on some silly girl who would prevent him from achieving the success he deserved.

'Bad move,' said Max laconically.

For the first time in his life, Gianni had looked at his mother with such cold distaste she'd faltered into silence, her tears drying on her cheeks in dismay. Then, with a bluntness that surprised his brother, Gianni had delivered the *coup de grâce* by announcing that he was already married, and to whom.

'For a moment I felt really sorry for her,' said Max. 'She

suddenly looked old and haggard. I was about to take off and leave them to it, when Luisa turned on me in fury and blamed *me* for encouraging Gianni to ruin his life.'

'Just as you said she would.'

'At this point Gianni interrupted and informed her that I'd known nothing about it until the day before. Luisa refused to believe it, of course,' said Max, 'so she delivered her own *coup de grâce* and told me I should have taken more care of Gianni because he is blood of my blood. According to Luisa, David Wingate is not my father.'

Abby gasped, and moved closer. 'Did you believe her?'

He let out a long, unsteady breath. 'At the time, no. But on the drive back it began to make more and more sense. Luisa's fiercely respectable Catholic parents banish her to relatives in London, where she marries David Wingate soon after she arrives there. Enzo disappears for a while, but when I meet him years later he treats me like his own son. It all adds up.'

'Even so, it doesn't make any difference, Max,' said Abby flatly. 'David is the father who brought you up. Remember what he said? Luisa was free to stay here in Italy. But he had no intention of letting her keep his son. *His* son, Max. Biological or not, David's your father in every way.' Some of her own tension lessened as she felt Max relax against her.

'I love you, Abby,' he said huskily. 'I don't know what I did to deserve someone so perfect, but God help anyone who tries to take you away from me.'

'I'm not perfect, Max,' she said in alarm.

'You are to me.' His voice deepened to a teasing note. 'Especially now I've solved your little problem.'

She dug him in the ribs. 'It was a big problem to me.'

'I know it was, my darling, and I solved it by crying all over you.' He kissed her swiftly. 'I haven't cried like that since I was ten—and Luisa was responsible that time, too.'

'Are you going to ask your father if she was telling the truth?'

'Yes. Not that his answer matters. To me, *he* is my father and always will be.' He gave a wry little laugh. 'But I was very fond of Enzo, too.'

'Then you're lucky,' said Abby firmly. 'You had Enzo as well as David in your life. I never knew my father. He died when I was little.'

'I know. And I sympathise with that.' He rubbed his cheek against hers. 'I can't do anything about a father for you, but I'm only too happy to provide you with a husband.'

Abby opened her eyes next morning to find Max propped on one elbow, watching her wake up.

'Good morning, darling,' he said. 'How did you sleep?'

She smiled sleepily. 'Like a log. Was I restless?'

'No idea—I slept like a log myself.'

'How do you feel today?'

'Due to expert counselling last night I'm in good mental shape,' he said, smiling, and turned back the covers.

'Not bad physical shape, either,' commented Abby, admiring his taut behind as he stood up.

Max paused, looking down at her with narrowed eyes. 'Was that an observation or an invitation?'

'Just a compliment,' she said hastily, and slid out of bed to snatch up her dressing gown. 'No point in looking at me like that. I'm—'

'Hungry!' he finished for her. 'Right. First one down makes the breakfast.'

'You're on.' Abby made for the door, then turned as she opened it. 'Are you all right, Max—really?'

He crossed the room in a few strides and took her in his arms. 'I'm a whole lot more than all right—I'm the luckiest man on the planet.'

When he let her go at last, Abby ran down to shower and dress in record time. Humming as she laid the table in the sunlit kitchen, she poured orange juice, and broke eggs into a bowl ready to whisk when Max appeared, newly shaved, and damp about the hair.

'What do you fancy?' she asked, smiling. 'Scrambled eggs or an omelette?'

'I won't say what I really fancy,' he told her, eyeing the snug fit of her jeans. 'But I'll eat whatever you cook. I'll do the toast and coffee.'

They discussed their plans for the day over a leisurely breakfast, Abby deeply relieved to see that all traces of Max's grief were gone. They lingered over the meal so long they were starting on a second pot of coffee when a car came zooming into the courtyard outside.

'That's Gianni's Lamborghini,' said Max, and went into the hall to open the front door. '*Com' estai?* How are things back at the ranch?'

'I have news too important to tell on the phone!' Gianni beamed as he hurried towards him. 'Rosa has brought in help to prepare a celebration lunch, and Mamma is getting dressed, ready to dazzle Papa Berni. Abby,' he added, and threw up his hands as she joined them, 'you are so beautiful this morning.'

'She's beautiful every morning,' said Max. 'Want some coffee?'

'*Grazie!*' said Gianni fervently. 'I need much help to get through this day. Rosa started cooking before dawn, when Mamma told her that Renata and her father are invited to eat with us.' He looked at Abby hopefully as they went to the kitchen. 'Perhaps you would both—?'

'No!' said Max flatly. 'I had enough yesterday.'

Gianni nodded, resigned. He shot a questioning look at Max as Abby filled a cup for him.

'I told her everything,' Max assured him.

'*Bene!* I am sure you gave him much comfort, Abby,' said Gianni, his eyes gleaming as she blushed to the roots of her hair.

Max pulled her down on his lap and kept her there. 'So what happened after I left?'

Gianni drank his coffee down with relish. 'I ordered Mamma to welcome Renata as her *nuora*.'

'Poor Luisa—presented with *two* daughters-in-law in one day; she must be wondering what hit her,' said Max. 'But how the devil did you get her to invite Renata and her father to lunch?'

Gianni smiled smugly. 'I told her that Mario Berni disapproved of Luisa Scotto's son as husband for his daughter.'

'Wow!' said Abby, as she got up to refill his cup. 'How did your mother take that?'

The black eyes rolled expressively. 'Not well.'

'I can imagine,' said Max dryly. 'So now, of course, she's hell-bent on showing Mario how lucky he is to have such a wonderful son-in-law.'

Gianni nodded cheerfully. 'But he is a sensible man. He knows that now Renata is my wife there is nothing he can do. When my beautiful bride arrives with him today she is bringing all her possessions.' His smile lit up the room. 'Tonight she sleeps at the Villa Falcone. With me.'

'Little brother, you're a brave man,' said Max with respect.

'*Allora*, that is enough about me.' Gianni eyed him with compassion. 'I must know how you feel. It is not right that Mamma said such things to you if they were not true.'

'After thinking it over I think they must be,' said Max, shrugging. 'But it's easy to prove.'

Gianni eyed him warily. 'If my father was also yours will you be unhappy?'

'Of course not. I was very fond of him.' Max grinned. 'The only drawback would be having you for a full brother instead of half!'

'It is not a drawback for me,' said Gianni simply.

Max's eyes softened as he returned his brother's hug, then

Gianni kissed Abby and rushed off to prepare for the momentous occasion.

'I'd like to be a fly on the wall at the lunch party,' said Abby as she cleared the table. She shot a look at Max. 'We should be there, you know, to show solidarity.'

'No,' he said flatly. 'Enough is enough. My idea in bringing you here this weekend was time spent alone with you.'

To Abby's delight it was warm enough later to sit by the long narrow pool. When Max stretched out on the chair next to her Abby gave a deep sigh of pleasure as she gazed down on the timeless panorama below.

'This is such a magical place. Yet in some ways, Max, I'm surprised that you chose to build your retreat here.'

'If Enzo hadn't left me the property I don't suppose I would have. But I'm half-Italian, remember? Possibly even wholly Italian,' he added, shrugging, and turned to look at her. 'Why the frown?'

'I was thinking about your father. But I won't talk about him if it still hurts.'

He reached out and took her hand to kiss it. 'It doesn't. Some wonderful medicine made me better.'

Abby felt hot and breathless at the mere thought of it. 'Look, darling, your father said he liked Enzo Falcone. And the three of you often dined together when Enzo was in London. If what Luisa said was true, would that have been possible for David?'

Max's eyes narrowed thoughtfully. 'It doesn't seem likely. But Dad's a very special man, so who knows? After my first visit here I didn't want to come back again, but he talked to me man to man, pointing out how much I would lose if I shut my mother—and Gianni—out of my life. And he was right.' His mouth tightened. 'If I'm honest, a major part of the problem with Luisa is my fault. I was bristling with teenage angst towards her during those first years at the Villa Falcone.

Due mainly to Enzo's influence—and some growing up—I gradually softened towards her, but after he died and she moved to Venice the gulf widened again.'

'Do you love her?' Abby demanded.

He blinked, then smiled crookedly. 'Yes, I suppose I do.'

She gave him a militant look. 'In that case, are you happy with the idea of Papa Berni looking down his nose at your mother?'

Max stiffened. 'No.' He shrugged impatiently. 'But there's nothing I can do about that.'

'Oh, yes, there is. We could turn up at the lunch to give our support.'

He stared at her incredulously. 'You seriously expect me to go another round with my lady mother today? No way. I had enough last night.'

'She was very upset last night, Max.'

'She wasn't the only one!' His jaw clenched. 'Can you begin to imagine how mortified I felt when you found me crying?'

Abby got up and slid onto his lap, relaxing into the arms which closed round her. 'Look at it another way, *fidanzato mio*. If you hadn't cried and I hadn't comforted you my famous problem would still be hanging over me, unsolved. In my opinion you should be grateful to your mother.'

He let out a snort of laughter and kissed her hard. 'Pure sophistry, Miss Green.'

'Soon to be Mrs Wingate,' she reminded him, and gave him a smile which made him blink. 'How much do you love me, Max?'

'So much I'll do anything you want,' he said gruffly. 'An admission I think I'm about to regret.'

Abby sat up straight on his lap, running a finger down his bare chest. 'You know exactly what I want.'

He sighed heavily. 'You think we should be there with Luisa and Gianni to close ranks against Mario Berni.'

'Yes. Please?'

'All right. You win. We'll go—but only to please you.'

'It will please your mother and Gianni, too.'

Max shook his head. 'Gianni, yes, but after last night I'm the last person Luisa wants at her party.'

Abby melted back into his arms, rubbing her cheek against his. 'I think you're wrong. Think about it logically. Enzo was the love of her life, and she says you are his son. Of course she wants you there. In her anguish over Gianni, she might have raged at you last night but she loves you, Max.'

'Damn funny way of showing it!' He tipped her face up to his. 'You're a dangerous woman, Abigail Green. Before I met you I thought of myself as a pretty tough customer. But one look from those eyes of yours and I melt like butter.'

Abby kissed him with passionate gratitude. 'Does that mean we're going?'

'You know it does.' He got up with her in his arms and set her on her feet, running a caressing hand down her back. 'I'll ring Gianni now.'

Abby watched him stride towards the house, devoutly hoping she'd done the right thing. But she'd seen the fleeting look of yearning in Luisa Falcone's eyes yesterday when she looked at Max. No matter what had passed between them later, it was time to mend fences.

Max came back, grinning broadly. 'Get your party dress on, then. I told a very excited Gianni not to say a word to Luisa. We'll arrive like the cavalry and save her day.'

Prepared for possible dining out in Todi, Abby had packed the topaz crêpe dress worn to the engagement party. 'Rachel works in a very expensive dress shop,' she told Max, presenting herself for inspection. 'She got this at a knock-down price for me, but the label is impressive, so is it the right sort of thing for the occasion?'

His eyes gleamed as they moved over her from top to toe. 'Perfect!'

Because it had been her bright idea to support Max's family at the celebration lunch, Abby felt she had no right to complain about a serious case of cold feet as they set off. Butterflies fluttered in her mid-section as she tried to talk normally on the way down the serpentine bends. What if she'd made a terrible mistake and Luisa was outraged by the sight of Max after the quarrel? Too late now, she thought numbly.

'What did you say?' she asked at one point, as she realised Max was eyeing her expectantly.

'You were miles away. Are you nervous, darling?'

'Shaking in my shoes,' she admitted.

'No wonder.' He glanced at her feet and laughed. 'How you can walk in those beats me.'

'I take taxis or drive.' She frowned. 'In London I had the use of a company car. But there's not much in the way of public transport in Stavely, and I can't keep borrowing Mother's Mini Cooper all the time, so I need a car. But,' she added, in sudden haste, 'don't even think of offering to buy me one.'

'I wouldn't dream of it,' he said innocently as they turned off on the road to the Villa Falcone.

Max spoke into the microphone at the gates, then drove on as Rosa buzzed him in. As they approached the house Abby felt a pang of sympathy when she saw a lone, elegant figure sitting bolt-upright on one of the antique rattan chairs on the loggia, a table set with drinks and canapés beside her. Luisa Falcone started to her feet, her eyes incredulous as Max emerged from the car. Abby felt him stiffen as he helped her out, and squeezed his hand encouragingly. He dropped a kiss on her hair then took her up the steps to join his mother.

'*Massimo?*' Luisa said apprehensively.

'*Buon giorno*, Mamma.' He hesitated for an instant, then embraced her gently. 'We thought you'd like some support today. Can you manage two extra for lunch?'

Two large tears welled in his mother's eyes as she returned

the embrace, and she sniffed hard, smiling gratefully as Abby handed her a tissue. *'Grazie,'* she said huskily, and reached up to touch her son's cheek, her eyes heavy with remorse. 'And thank you also, *mio figlio*. Can you find it in your heart to forgive me, Max? In my anger at Gianni I was so cruel to you last night. You have told Abigail this?'

'Yes. She knows it all.'

Luisa offered her cheek for Abby's kiss. 'I think it was you who persuaded Max to come. After what I said to him last night—' She paused a moment, swallowing hard. 'I thought I would never see him again.'

'I didn't want to at first,' said Max frankly. 'But Abby reminded me that Mario Berni disapproves of your son for his daughter, and no one is allowed to disapprove of my family.'

'Grazie!' Luisa gave him a look of such blazing gratitude his eyes softened as he patted her cheek.

'It's Abby's influence, Mamma. She made me see that it's time to put our differences in the past where they belong.'

'Then I am deeply grateful to you, *cara*,' said Luisa, blinking away tears as she embraced Abby.

'Go inside and do your face again, Mamma,' said Max. 'You must look your best when your guests arrive.'

'E vero!' She squared her shoulders. 'I must tell Rosa you are here, and also fetch something from my room. Give Abby a glass of wine, *tesoro*.'

Max smiled as he watched his mother hurry into the house. 'It's a long time since she called me that.'

'You were magnificent,' said Abby, impressed. 'She was so afraid when she saw you, but once you said Mamma she lit up like a Christmas tree.'

'All down to you, my darling,' he assured her, and poured the wine. He handed her a glass, then raised his own in toast. 'Here's to Luisa, and to Gianni and Renata, and, most important of all, to us.'

'To all of us,' said Abby thankfully.

Luisa hurried back to them, her face flawless again. 'Perhaps you would prefer something new, Abby, but, Max, this is for you to give to your beautiful *fidanzata* if you would like to. Your father gave it to me.'

'Which father?' he asked bluntly, taking the ring she was holding out.

'David, *naturalmente*.' She took his hand, squaring her shoulders as she turned to Abby. 'There are things which must be said before the others arrive. It is hard to believe now, but Max was very small when he was born. It was many weeks before we could take him home.' She blinked furiously to check more tears. 'The doctors said he was premature. If they were right he was David's son; if not he could have been Enzo's. I don't know. They did not have the DNA test then.'

'So why did you fling that at me last night?' demanded Max.

'Because I am a stupid, spiteful woman!' she said bitterly. 'But when I calmed down I felt much remorse. I know well it is not your fault that Gianni is married to Renata Berni.' Luisa shrugged wryly. 'Besides, who am I to complain? I come from even humbler stock than hers.'

Abby turned at the sound of cars winding their way up to the gate. 'Is that Gianni's?'

'One of them. Papa Berni must be driving his own car,' said Max, examining the beautiful diamond solitaire his mother had given him. He gave Abby a questioning look, then at her eager nod slid the ring on her finger.

'It fits?' said Luisa anxiously.

'It's perfect,' said Max, with a grin for Abby. 'So, my darling. Do you like it?'

'I love it!' She smiled radiantly as she kissed Max and then turned to kiss his mother. 'It's not only a glorious ring; it means so much because it once belonged to you. Thank you.'

Luisa flushed with pleasure. 'I tried to give it back to David after—after we parted, but he said it was my keepsake of our time together. You have met him, Abby?'

'I have indeed. I like him very much.'

Luisa smiled fondly. 'So do I. Always.'

'But you loved Enzo.'

'From when we were children.' Her face shadowed. 'I still do.' She took in a deep breath as the Lamborghini drew up, followed by a larger saloon car packed with luggage.

Max moved to stand between his mother and Abby with an arm round each waist. 'Smile, Mamma,' he whispered.

Luisa looked up at him with gratitude, her smile bright as she walked down the steps to kiss Renata and hold out her hand to Mario Berni, who bent over it with stiff formality. They exchanged a few stilted words, then Luisa led him up the steps and in slow, deliberate English introduced Abby and renewed his acquaintance with Max.

Holding his bride by the hand, Gianni came up the steps to embrace Abby, whispering fervent thanks in her ear for softening Max's heart, but she shook her head.

'He wanted to be here for you,' she assured him, and embraced Renata, who looked ravishing in a pale pink dress, but so dazed and nervous it would have been a hard heart that refused to welcome her.

The superb meal was served under a pergola in the sunshine, and with the help of Rosa's food and some of the choicest vintages from Enzo Falcone's cellar the party went on so long into the evening, Abby dozed in the car on the way home.

'Sorry about that, Max,' she said, yawning as the car turned into the courtyard. 'But it was a triumph today. Aren't you glad you made the effort?'

'Of course I am. You were absolutely right to insist we turned up. No way was I going to let Mario Berni—or anyone else—look down on my family.' He laughed suddenly. 'Though by the time we left old Mario was so mellow with good food and wine he was eating out of Luisa's hand and praising Gianni to me as the best tenor in Italy.'

Abby chuckled. 'It was such a brilliant idea of yours to ask Gianni to sing after lunch. If your mother had still harboured any doubts about Renata, they vanished for ever when she accompanied him so exquisitely on the piano.'

'True. In fact the only sticky moment of the day was when Gianni insisted Rosa ate lunch with us. But Luisa never batted an eyelid, so Mario was forced into a truce with his sister-in-law. Apparently he was furious with Rosa after she connived at the secret wedding. Why are you smiling?' asked Max as they went in the house.

'I was just wondering what you can think up for my next visit,' said Abby, kicking off her shoes. 'It would have to be something pretty spectacular to outdo this weekend!'

'Easy!' Max took her in his arms. 'Next trip will be our honeymoon.'

'Wonderful. But we have to get married first.' She shivered suddenly.

'You're cold,' said Max quickly. 'I'll light the fire.'

'It's a bit late for that. We've got an early start tomorrow, so let's just go to bed and talk over the party like an old married couple.'

'Brilliant idea,' said Max, and kissed her. 'You go up and do what you have to do. I'll be up soon.'

Once her night-time ritual was over, Abby pondered a moment, then put on the brief lawn nightgown she kept for travelling and went up to the master bedroom to find the master still missing. She switched on lamps, put her dressing gown on a chair, propped up the pillows and got into bed to lean against them.

Max arrived a moment later, backing in with a tray of drinks.

'I brought your water and some fruit juice, but if you ask me nicely I'll go back down and make some coffee,' he offered.

Abby shook her head. 'No coffee at this time of night. Next time I come I'll bring tea bags.'

He eyed her nightgown, but made no comment as he went off to the bathroom. When he came back he was wearing boxers. 'I gather it's an occasion to dress up for tonight,' he remarked as he got in beside her.

'It's not an irreversible situation,' said Abby, batting her eyelashes. 'But I wanted to talk for a while before we go to sleep. And even someone of my limited experience, Max Wingate, knows there's fat chance of that with nothing on.'

He laughed, and took her hand as he leaned back against the pillows beside her. 'What shall we talk about?'

'If it's not too private, I'd like to know what you and your mother were chatting about so animatedly just before we left.'

'I was inviting her to stay at my place in Pennington.'

'But that's wonderful, Max! I thought she wouldn't fly.'

'When I told her she could get to the wedding by train it was a done deal—and she intends asking Gianni to sing during the service.'

'We can't ask him to do that,' protested Abby.

'Luisa insists. She's been cheated out of his wedding, so she thinks he should help to make everything wonderful for ours.'

'And will Gianni agree?'

'Now his *mamma* has welcomed Renata into the family, Gianni will do anything she wants.' Max moved closer. 'But let's talk about what I want.'

Abby turned to face him, smiling expectantly. 'What *do* you want?'

'You!'

CHAPTER ELEVEN

TORRENTIAL rain on the drive to Florence caused so much delay next day, they arrived at the airport with barely enough time to make their flight. There was turbulence most of the way to Stansted, and such heavy rain on the drive back to Stavely that Max stayed only long enough to see Abby inside Briar Cottage and exchange a swift greeting with Isabel before setting off for Pennington on the last lap of the journey.

Isabel ordered her travel-weary daughter to sit down, and put the kettle on.

'I'm dying for some tea,' said Abby gratefully. 'I must take some with me next time.'

'So there will be a next time, then?'

'Definitely.' Abby's heavy eyes sparkled suddenly. 'In fact, Mrs Green, our next trip there will be our honeymoon. Max's mother handed over the ring his father gave her. We're officially engaged.' She held out her hand, and Isabel blinked hard as she bent to hug her.

'Darling, I'm so happy for you.' She smiled, sniffing as she admired the ring. 'Max didn't take long to persuade you, then.'

'I didn't need much persuading. I asked him round tomorrow night for your official blessing, but don't worry, I'll cook.'

Abby talked non-stop while her mother poached eggs and made toast as she listened, enthralled, to the story of Gianni and Renata and the celebration lunch. When Abby had finished her supper and could talk no more without yawning, Isabel shooed her off to bed, then snapped her fingers as Abby kissed her goodnight.

'In all the excitement I forgot my own piece of news. I've heard about a job you might like—if you still want one, of course.'

'Can you see me as a Stepford Wife? Of course I want a job. What is it?'

'On Saturday I met Colonel Granger, your old boss at Millwood House, and his ears pricked up when he heard you were job-hunting in Pennington. Apparently Mrs Ellison, his administration assistant, wants to retire. He hasn't started advertising for a replacement yet, so the Colonel thought you might like to have a chat with him before he puts the wheels in motion.'

Abby threw her arms round her mother in excitement. 'Millwood House is only a few miles from Pennington. It would be wonderful to work there again.'

'Will you move in with Max straight away?'

'No. He wants me to, but I'd rather wait until we're married.'

Isabel shook her head in wonder. 'This is a lot to take in. How long do I get to plan a wedding?'

'That's one of the things Max wants to discuss tomorrow. He's keen to get married soon—me too.' Abby coloured slightly. 'So first thing in the morning I'll ring Laura and put her in the picture, and then I'll get in touch with Colonel Granger.'

'You'd better tell Rachel too.'

'Lord, yes. I'll ring before she leaves for work tomorrow.'

Rachel was wild with excitement when she heard the news. 'We could have a double wedding!'

'And have you outshine me? No, thanks!'

'As if I could! At least come and buy your dress at the shop. I'll get Heloise to knock a big chunk off the price.'

'An offer I can't refuse. Must dash. You need to get to work and I must ring Laura.'

'You rang me first?' said Rachel huskily. 'That's so sweet of you, Abby. Let's get together soon.'

'Actually, I thought I might come in later today. I'll ring when I'm on my way so you can sneak off and have a coffee with me.'

Laura was as delighted as Rachel. 'Are you happy, love? Really happy, I mean?'

'Yes. Really. I'm very lucky.'

'I think Max is the lucky one. I'll ring Domenico right now, and warn him I want the most fabulous outfit in Venice.'

'Not much problem finding one there! Will Isabella fancy being a bridesmaid?'

'Will she! She'll be thrilled to bits. So am I. How's Mother taking it?'

'She's delighted. We'll discuss details with Max over dinner tonight, but right now I'm driving her to school so I can borrow the car. Talk to you later.' Abby handed the phone to her mother for a brief word, then rushed her out to the car. 'Can't let the Head set a bad example!'

When Abby got back to the cottage she found a message asking if she could manage to get in to see Colonel Granger at ten-thirty, and rang back at once to say she could.

Abby rushed upstairs to touch up her face and coil her hair in a sleek, shining twist, then exchanged her trainers and jeans for slim black heels and pale grey jacket and pencil-skirt and ran back to the car. She made such good time on the journey along the major route that once she turned off at the sign for Millwood House she was able to cruise slowly along the familiar road that wound through parkland inhabited by deer clustered under trees already bright with the flamboyant colours of autumn. When the graceful Palladian façade came into view Abby drove past the main house and parked outside the stable block which housed the restaurant and administration offices.

Abby knocked on the door of the reception office and went in, smiling to find Mrs Ellison talking to Colonel Granger.

'Well, well,' he said, his keen blue eyes twinkling. 'Is this vision of elegance really little Abigail?'

Abby laughed and held out her hand to them both in turn 'Present and correct, sir—though I was never very little. It's lovely to see you both again.'

The Colonel turned to Mrs Ellison. 'Ask the restaurant for coffee for three, please, Mrs E, and then sit in on the interview. I'll need your input.'

The interview was very different from Abby's encounter with the hedge managers. That trio of clever, flippant young men had made it very plain they found her physically attractive as well as suited to their requirements for the job. But Colonel Granger and Mrs Ellison had known her since she was a schoolgirl, something she realised once the interview was underway, which might not act in her favour if they were after someone older. But she banked on the fact that the work she'd done for Hadley Enterprises, coupled with her academic qualifications and her previous familiarity with Millwood House, would convince her kindly interrogators she was more than capable of helping Colonel Granger with its administration.

'We've branched out a bit lately,' he informed her. 'Must keep up with the times and diversify to keep the place running. We still do concerts, of course, both the outdoor picnic type and the indoor version in the Great Hall. And since you were here last the lodges at three of the entrance gates have been converted into smart holiday lets.'

'And we do complete package weddings now, too,' Mrs Ellison reminded him. 'They're a relatively new departure, but a very good source of revenue.'

'I wonder you can bear to retire, Mrs E,' said Abby. 'It all sounds so exciting.'

'Tiring, too, dear. It needs younger blood than mine.' She glanced at the Colonel, who returned the look steadily for a moment, then smiled as he turned to Abby.

'Because Millwood House is autonomous, and not part of the National Trust, I'm able to trust to my own judgement when taking on staff, particularly someone who's worked here in the past. I know I speak for Mrs Ellison when I say you seem eminently suited to the job, Abby, so I take great pleasure in offering you the post.'

'Thank you very much indeed, Colonel,' she said, thrilled. 'I'm delighted to accept.'

'When could you start, dear?' said Mrs Ellison, once a contract had been produced for Abby to sign.

'Right away,' Abby assured her. 'Tomorrow morning, if you like.' She hesitated. 'But before I sign there's something you should both know. It seems rather a cheek to ask for time off before I even start, but I'm getting married soon. I'll need two weeks off next month for a honeymoon.'

Rachel was seeing a customer off the premises when she saw Abby hurrying down the street. She threw her arms round her friend, drew her inside the shop and closed the door. 'Gosh, you look frighteningly elegant today. Come on, then, show me the ring—wow, what a rock!'

'It has sentimental value, too,' said Abby, looking at it fondly. 'It belonged to Max's mother. Can you nip out for a bit right now?'

Rachel hurried off to tell a colleague she was taking her lunch break early, then put a coat over her smart dress and thrust her arm through Abby's, demanding all her news as they left the shop. Once they were settled in the nearest of the numerous coffee shops that had opened up all over town in recent years, Rachel reported on her own wedding plans, then smiled guiltily.

'I forgot to ask,' she said, pausing to take breath. 'Tell me about this interview.'

Abby described the post at Millwood House and smiled triumphantly. 'I've got the job!'

'Of course you have, and they're jolly lucky to get you. Congratulations! Now, then,' Rachel added. 'When are you coming in to look at wedding dresses?'

Abby grinned. 'Trust you to get your priorities right! But I'll talk to Max tonight before I start thinking about dresses.'

'Whatever you fancy we've either got it or Heloise will hunt it down,' Rachel assured her, and beamed suddenly as she spotted a man in formal black looking round the coffee shop.

'Marcus!' She waved vigorously.

He strode towards them, smiling. 'Good morning, ladies. Your boss told me you'd be here, Rachel.' He bent to kiss his sister's cheek. 'May I join you?'

'Of course,' said Rachel happily, and beckoned to the waitress.

'Hi, Marcus,' said Abby. 'Shouldn't you be in London, prosecuting someone?'

'I'm doing that in court right here this week, unless I can wrap it up sooner. I just popped out for some lunch.' He smiled. 'And how are you, Abby? Rachel tells me congratulations are in order.'

She smiled serenely. 'Yes. Thank you.'

'I take it you're marrying the possessive man you brought to Rachel's party?'

Abby nodded. 'Max Wingate.'

Marcus smiled as the waitress asked for their order. 'I've got a few minutes. I'll get another round of coffees.'

Rachel shook her head regretfully. 'Not for me. I must get back. But treat Abby to another so she can tell you all about her new job.'

'Actually, I must be off too,' said Abby quickly.

'Stay for a while; relax while you can,' ordered Rachel. 'You'll be hard at work soon enough tomorrow. Ring me and tell me how you get on. Will you pay for me, Marcus?' She kissed them both and hurried out of the café.

'She never changes,' said Marcus indulgently. 'You know, Abigail, it amazes me that you and Rachel have always been thick as thieves. You're poles apart in every single way except age.'

'I love her,' said Abby simply.

'So do I. She's a darling, but you must admit she's never been academic.'

'What does that matter? She enjoys her job and her life, and she's going to marry a man who adores her and will make her happy.'

Marcus smiled. 'You should come and argue my case for me. You'd win!'

She returned the smile politely. 'Will you win today?'

'Oh, yes. This week, if not today. Tell me about this new job.'

Abby gave a brief description of the post, then stood up. 'I won't wait for the coffee. I have shopping to do, Marcus, so I'd better be on my way.'

'An unexpected pleasure to see you again, Abigail. Pass on my congratulations to Wingate. Tell him he's a very lucky man.' He got up and took her hand, his eyes sober as they met hers. 'I envy him.'

Abby raised an eyebrow in disbelief as she said goodbye, and left the café to head for the food hall of the biggest department store in town. When she got back to Stavely at last, she backed the Mini behind a chunky four-wheel-drive vehicle outside Briar Cottage and took her shopping round the back of the house to find her mother sitting at the kitchen table, drinking tea with a man new to Abby.

'Hello, darling,' said Isabel cheerfully. 'I read your note.

This is Lewis Clive, who keeps the garden in shape for me. Lewis, meet my daughter Abigail.'

The visitor got up to shake Abby's hand, blue eyes smiling in an attractive, deeply tanned face. 'A pleasure to meet you at last. I've heard a lot about you.'

'Really?' Abby smiled politely.

Isabel eyed Abby's appearance expectantly. 'Did you get in touch with the Colonel?'

'I certainly did. I went to Millwood House for an interview and got the job,' said Abby jubilantly.

'Goodness, that was quick!' Isabel got up to hug her. 'I'm so glad for you, I know you've been a bit edgy with time on your hands. When do you start?'

'Nine in the morning.'

'As soon as that?'

'I'd better be off and let you celebrate,' said Lewis Clive quickly. 'Hearty congratulations to you, Abby. I hope we meet again soon.'

'I'll see you out,' said Isabel, and went outside with him to the car.

Abby began putting the food away, her eyes thoughtful. When her mother came back, she gave her a teasing look. 'A gardener who calls you by your first name, Mrs Green?'

To her daughter's surprise, Isabel flushed. 'Lewis owns the garden services firm I told you about.'

'Ah, so he doesn't do the dirty work himself, then!'

'He comes along to check the job done by his crew. Lewis sees to the landscaping and administration side of the business. He used to work in the City, but at some stage he decided to get out of the financial rat-race, indulge his passion for gardening and start up the firm.' Isabel paused. 'Since Lewis moved into Down End a few months ago we've become quite good friends.'

'So that's where you went to lunch.' Abby eyed her mother thoughtfully. 'Did his wife move in with him?'

'No. She married someone else years ago.'

Abby took off her jacket and slung it on a chair. 'You've kept him pretty quiet.'

'I wanted you to meet him before I told you about him.' Isabel met her daughter's eyes very directly. 'I wasn't sure how you'd react.'

'So you're more than just good friends, then?'

Isabel hesitated, then shrugged, smiling. 'I suppose you could say that.'

Abby sat down with a thump, her eyes wide. 'Max was right.'

'About what?'

'Your sex-life.'

'I beg your pardon?' Isabel flushed indignantly. 'Why on earth were you discussing a thing like that with Max?'

Abby jumped up to hug her mother. 'Because I had such difficulties with my own sex-life and Max thought I should confide in you about it. Don't be cross.'

'I'm embarrassed, not cross.' Isabel paused, frowning, and touched a gentle hand to her daughter's cheek. 'Are you still having difficulties, love?'

'Not any more.' Abby smiled dreamily. 'This weekend I learned that the problem just needed the right man to solve it.'

'And Max is the right man, of course.' Isabel hugged her daughter in relief. 'I knew that the moment I laid eyes on him. And, talking of Max, shouldn't we be doing something about dinner?'

'Yes, but first enlighten me, Mother dear. Does Lewis want to marry you?'

Isabel gave her daughter a saucy grin. 'I hope not, at least not yet. I rather enjoy being courted.' She bit her lip. 'How do you think Laura will react?'

'The same as me. Surprise first, then pleasure because you're happy. And if Lewis Clive makes you happy that's all that matters.' Abby rolled up her shirtsleeves and tied on an apron. 'Enough of this emoting. I really must crack on with the beef Wellington.'

'Good heavens, is that what you have in mind?' said Isabel in alarm. 'I've never attempted that.'

'Neither have I. Look on it as an adventure. We can always open a tin of beans if it goes wrong!'

Nothing went wrong, which was no surprise to Abby. This was a day for everything to go right. While Isabel did the potatoes and made a salad dressing, Abby put the main dish together herself. With an open cookery-book in front of her, she seared a fillet of beef, sautéed mushrooms, shallots and garlic in the juices left in the pan, let the mixture cool, then spread it on the meat, sealed the result in puff pastry and put it in a hot oven, timed to be ready when Max arrived.

He came punctually, laden with champagne and roses for Isabel, and Abby ran downstairs into the arms he held out to catch her.

'I've got a job!' she said, after he'd put her down.

'Since last night?' he said, laughing.

'Mother had it all organised for me,' Abby explained jubilantly, and took him by the hand to pull him into the kitchen. 'How's my Wellington?'

'I haven't dared check,' confessed Isabel, absorbed in arranging a great sheaf of apricot roses in a vase. 'Just look at these beauties. You're very extravagant, Max.'

'Next time you get daisies, Isabel,' he warned, grinning. 'Tonight is a special occasion.'

'That it is,' said Abby, bending to open the oven. 'Hey, this looks good, if I do say so myself.'

It was a triumphant success. Abby served the thick slices of rare beef in their flaking pastry crust with a simple accompaniment of green salad and new potatoes, and waited, tense, for Max's comments as he tasted the first mouthful.

'Perfect,' he said, eyes closed in rapture.

'His favourite word,' she told her mother, resigned.

Max opened his eyes and smiled. 'With regard to your daughter, Isabel, it invariably fits the bill!'

Over dinner Isabel reminded them that banns had to be called, which meant that, much to Max's regret, a date seven weeks later was the earliest possible for the wedding ceremony. And even then it had to be left fluid for the moment, to make sure Gianni was free.

'Will your Colonel be happy while you're away?' asked Max later, when Isabel had tactfully taken herself off to bed.

'Oh, yes. Mrs Ellison isn't leaving until after Christmas.' Abby smiled at him in wonder. 'I can't believe this is happening at all, Max, let alone going so smoothly.'

'Then allow me to convince you, my darling,' he said, and kissed her very thoroughly.

When he raised his head Abby sighed. 'Max, will you do something for me?'

'Anything you want.'

'Stop thinking of me as perfect. I'm not, never was, and can't hope to be in future. You must take me as I am, with all faults.'

He grinned, but sobered quickly when he saw she was deadly serious. 'I haven't discovered any faults yet, but you're right. No one's perfect. God knows I'm not. So I promise to love you just the way you are, Abigail Green. Almost perfect.'

'Good. I promise to love you the same way, Max Wingate.' Abby moved away slightly, her eyes dancing. 'Now I can tell you something I've been bursting to pass on all evening, but I had to wait until we were alone.'

Max eyed her narrowly. 'Will I like it?'

'Probably. It certainly proves you right. Today I met the man responsible for keeping the garden in shape.'

He eyed her narrowly. 'But you knew Isabel had help, so what's the big deal? Didn't you like him?'

'I only met him for a few minutes, but I liked what I saw. Which is a good thing, because he's a friend of Mother's—a very close friend,' she added significantly.

'How close is "close"?' he demanded.

Abby grinned as she explained the situation. 'Though in my opinion Mother's happy for him to come courting because it solves the problem of what to do with her retirement.'

'I'll recommend the idea to my father! He sends his love, by the way. I spoke to him earlier, but I didn't bring up the paternity question over the phone. He's coming down to Pennington for the weekend on Friday. Can you have dinner with us?'

Abby shook her head. 'You have your evening with David while I recover from my first few days at Millwood House. I'll join you for lunch on Saturday. Or you could bring him here to meet Mother.'

'Why don't you both come in on Saturday, and I'll treat you to lunch at the Chesterton?'

'Done. If she's free, of course.'

'Keep me posted.' Max pulled her onto his lap. 'In the meantime, I need a lot of tender loving care right now, *fidanzata mia*, to see me through until Saturday. Tomorrow and Thursday my presence is required at working dinners to further the cause of WLS. What will you do, Abby?'

'I did have a life before I met you, Max Wingate,' she teased. 'I'll spend the time recovering from earning my living again.'

'You're sure you'll be happy at Millwood House?'

'Absolutely.' She smiled wryly. 'Just between you and me, I didn't fancy any of the openings Pennington had to offer.'

'So what will you actually do?'

'I'll have a finger in all sorts of pies as Assistant Administrator. I've done some of it before, in a more lowly capacity, but this time I'll be the power behind the Colonel's throne, making sure the place runs like clockwork.'

'Can you manage that and still have energy left over to organise our wedding?' he demanded.

'Of course.' Abby smiled triumphantly. 'A good administrator always gets her priorities right.'

'Excellent. In that case, stop talking and kiss me, woman.'

After her first day back at Millwood House Abby felt as though she'd never been away. Colonel Granger took her round the staff to renew her acquaintance with old friends and introduce her to the new faces, and afterwards Abby explored the house with Mrs Ellison, and took note of all the changes. Later she shared a sandwich lunch with her mentor at her desk while she learned from the source of all knowledge how Millwood House functioned

'By the time you're flying solo, this will all be second nature to you,' Mrs Ellison assured her. 'You did all kinds of jobs here when you came down from Cambridge. I seem to remember you even waited on tables in the restaurant during some crisis or other.'

'Anyone who needed a hand usually got me,' said Abby, chuckling. 'Simon Hadley, the events organiser, was one of the people I was assigned to, which was very lucky for me because it eventually led to the job with him.'

'That reminds me, we've a gala concert scheduled in two weeks' time,' said Mrs Ellison. 'Your input with that will be much appreciated. They were hoping to get that new Italian tenor, but he wasn't free.'

'If you mean Giancarlo Falcone, he's in such demand I had quite a struggle to tie him down for Hadley Enterprises next summer,' agreed Abby, and smiled demurely. 'But just between you and me, Mrs E, he's going to sing at my wedding.'

The other woman stared at her in amazement. 'How on earth did you manage that?'

'He's my fiancé's half-brother, and his mother insists on

it. Though Gianni's so good-natured he's happy to do it as long as we choose a date when he's free. What is it, Mrs E?' she added as the woman stared at her in excitement.

'Where are you getting married, dear?'

'In the church in Stavely. We're waiting to hear from Gianni before we fix the actual date.'

'If you haven't arranged it yet, why not have the wedding here?' Mrs Ellison called up a window on the computer and scrolled down a list of dates. 'There. You can have most of November, or very early December. Christmas is more difficult, because so much goes on here during the festive season. We have a wedding here this very Friday, so you can see whether the idea appeals. If you do decide on it, your mother needn't worry about a thing. All the arrangements can be done here—ceremony, wedding breakfast, flowers, cake, champagne, even the transport. All you have to do is buy a dress and organise someone to accompany the soloist on our very fine Bechstein grand piano.'

'No problem there. Gianni's talented bride will do that for free.'

'How marvellous!' Mrs Ellison's eyes were dreamy for a moment before her practical side got the upper hand again. 'And just think of the advantages if it's a wet day!'

'What do you think of the idea, Mother?' said Abby when she got home that night. 'Are you dead set on a church wedding?'

'My darling child, it's your day, and your choice—and Max's, of course.' Isabel smiled. 'And Max won't mind how or where you get married as long as it's soon.'

This was something Max agreed to fervently when she rang him before he took off for one of his dinners. 'It sounds good to me. Just make it soon.'

'I'll do my best. Have a good time tonight.'

'Fat chance! My idea of a good time,' he said, in a tone

which rocketed her blood pressure, 'is a cosy little supper for two right here, followed by a move to my nice big bed, where I make love to you all night.'

'Oh, yes, please!'

'Fighting talk at the other end of a phone! Let's see if you're still brave on Sunday, after my father leaves.' He paused. 'Much as I want to see him, I wish Dad wasn't coming this weekend. It means a hell of a long wait before I get you to myself again.'

Next morning Abby buttonholed the Colonel as soon as she got in. 'My mother disapproves of my cycling to work, so do you have any recommendations about local used-car dealers, Colonel? I can't keep using my mother's car.'

He looked surprised. 'You should have mentioned your transport problem before. I took it for granted that the smart Mini was yours.'

'Unfortunately not. I really must get one of my own.'

'Until you do, how do you feel about driving a van with the Millwood House logo on it?'

She grinned in delight. 'I'd love it! That would be a huge help.'

'Right. Ring the Estate Office, tell them to get one overhauled for you, ready for tomorrow.'

By the end of the day Abby felt she was beginning to get to grips with the complex job. Under the stern tutelage of Mrs Ellison she steadily became familiar with the minutiae of caring for Millwood House. During the day she took two bookings for the holiday lets, made an appointment for a couple to inspect Millwood as a suitable place for a wedding, chased up deliveries the restaurant was desperate for, and checked all the details for the forthcoming concert, happy that there, at least, she was on familiar ground.

Isabel was waiting for the car to arrive, dressed ready to

go out, when Abby finally got home. She chuckled when she heard about the van.

'How kind of Colonel Granger. Though I'm perfectly happy for you to go on using the Mini.'

'I know, and I'm grateful, but I can't keep holding you up like this. My own transport is a much better idea all round. What's in your social diary this evening?'

'Supper for two with Lewis at Down End. Raid the fridge for your own. I've put a list of possible menus on the door.' Isabel kissed her. 'Don't wait up,' she called as she hurried to the car.

Abby felt restless as she listened to a message on her phone telling her Max would ring her when he got home. What could she do to pass the time until then? The same thing she did before she met him, she told herself scornfully, and went off to put some supper together. Afterwards she tried Sadie's number, and to her relief her friend answered.

'At last,' said Abby. 'I've been trying to contact you for days. I'm tired of listening to your machine.'

'I've been away on a shoot for a new promotion. Just got through the door, actually. Why didn't you leave a message?'

'I wanted to tell you my news in person. Are you ready for this? I'm getting married!'

Sadie gave a scream of excitement, then fired questions until she was satisfied she knew everything. 'Does this mean you've sorted yourself out, love?' she said delicately.

'Max did that. I'm so happy, Sadie.'

'Wonderful news. I'll pop into Harvey Nicks tomorrow for a hat!'

The chimes of Big Ben were heralding the Ten o'clock News when Abby heard a rap on the front door. She frowned. Too early for her mother. And not many people came visiting at this hour.

'Who's there?' she called, in answer to a second tattoo on the door.

'Max. Let me in.'

She flung open the door, her delighted smile fading abruptly as she saw his face. 'What's wrong? Was your dinner cancelled?'

'No. It finished early.'

Max closed the door behind him, and because it was obvious that he wasn't going to kiss her any time soon Abby returned to her sofa, alarm bells clanging in her head.

'Would you like coffee, or a drink?'

'Neither.' He leaned against the chimney piece, immaculate as always in a dark formal suit, his shirt as crisp as though he'd just put it on, his eyes as hard as iron.

Abby took in a deep breath. 'Something is obviously very wrong indeed. So tell me what it is, please, before you worry me to death.'

'I'd like some answers.'

Her eyes narrowed. 'To what questions, exactly?'

'First, I'll tell you who I met tonight. Marcus Kent was among the legal fraternity invited to the dinner. Apparently he's in court here this week. He made a point of latching on to me before the meal to congratulate me on our engagement, and to let me know how much he'd enjoyed having coffee with you recently.' Max paused. 'You didn't tell me about that.'

Abby shrugged. 'It wasn't exactly earth-shattering news. I met Rachel for coffee, and Marcus merely joined us for a few minutes.'

The dark eyes bored into hers. 'He took enormous pleasure in telling me about the endearing crush you once had on him, and how he'd been flattered and very much aware of it. As a leggy teenager, apparently, you would have tempted a saint. Which, he stressed, he was not. And, now you've matured into a beautiful woman, he hopes I appreciate how lucky I am.'

'Is that all?' she asked quietly.

Max shrugged. 'I got the impression he'd said everything

he wanted to say, and felt good about it, but there was nothing—nothing obvious, at least—that I could object to.'

'You could have rung to tell me something so trivial, surely?'

'I needed to see you face to face to ask the question I look on as bloody important, not trivial,' he snapped. 'Tell me the truth, Abby. Was Marcus Kent the "boy" who raped you?'

Abby stared at him in silence for a moment, then shrugged wearily. 'Yes, he was.'

Max looked sick. 'Why the hell didn't you report it?'

'How could I? He was Rachel's brother—besides, it wasn't rape.'

His fists clenched. 'When a man several years older forces his sister's teenage schoolfriend to have sex with him, how else would you describe it?'

She looked up at him. 'As he so rightly said, I had this huge crush on him at the time, so there was no force involved in the beginning.'

'Tell me exactly what happened.'

Abby eyed him in disbelief. 'You actually want the *details*?'

'Yes,' he snapped. 'Everything.'

She shrugged. 'If you must know, I was quite thrilled when he started kissing me. The boys I knew didn't fancy me, so this was new in my life. Because it was new, I was clueless about how quickly things can get out of hand. For once, I was wearing a skirt, and when he started tearing at my underwear I was shocked rigid and tried to fight him off. Bad move. It seemed to excite him even more. Marcus is not a small man, so when he got on top of me I couldn't push him off. I felt a searing pain and soon afterwards he collapsed on me like a dead weight, gasping out apologies, and it was all over.'

Max sat down suddenly, as though someone had cut him off at the knees. 'Does he know what effect it had on you afterwards?'

'Of course not,' she said scornfully.

'Did you see him again?'

'No. He was based in London and I went up to Cambridge soon afterwards, so it was easy to make sure our paths rarely crossed. Rachel's engagement party was one of the few times when they did.'

'At which point Marcus Kent found that you were even more of a temptation grown up, and he was hot to repeat the original experience,' said Max harshly. 'If he'd tried again would he have succeeded?'

'You mean that now I've tasted the delights of sex with you I might fancy it with Marcus as well?' Her eyes blazed with fierce distaste. 'If so, you couldn't be more wrong. I will never, ever let him touch me for one very good reason. That horrible, painful fiasco made me pregnant. Do you think I would let it happen again?'

CHAPTER TWELVE

THE colour drained from Max's face. 'You had his child?' he said hoarsely.

Her mouth twisted. 'Not for long.'

'You mean you had it adopted?'

'No, I lost it.' Abby hugged her arms across her chest, shuddering at the memory. 'I was distraught when I found I was pregnant. I'd never had a boyfriend, so a baby would have been hard to explain. Suddenly, due to Marcus, I was faced with giving up my place at Trinity, and my life was in pieces. Rachel was my usual confidante, so I couldn't tell a soul what was wrong. After weeks of misery, I finally told Mother I was spending Sunday with Rachel and caught the coach to London, to ask Laura to help me get a termination.'

Max winced. 'And did she?'

'She had no idea how to go about it, and fortunately she didn't have to. I felt so awful on the journey I thought that the pregnancy test had been wrong and I was starting a period after all. Looking back, I can't believe I was so stupid. I somehow made it to Laura's flat in Bow, just in time to part with my little burden.' Abby looked away. 'And cried my heart out when it was all over.'

Max swallowed. 'You were *sorry* you lost his child?'

'No. The tears were hormonal,' she snapped. 'Once they'd dried I was euphoric.'

'The bastard should be made to pay for the harm he did,' said Max savagely.

Abby glared at him. 'Absolutely not!'

'You're *protecting* him?'

'You're not thinking straight,' she said scathingly. 'I'm protecting Rachel and Mrs Kent, not Marcus. They both adore him. And in all fairness he's a good son and brother. What happened with me was a one-off, an accident that happened in the past. And it's going to stay in the past.'

'Even though the bastard gave you an aversion to sex that could have ruined your life?' demanded Max, and jumped to his feet to stride around the kitchen, looking like a panther baulked of its prey. 'If I'd known this tonight I'd have beaten him to a pulp.'

'That's your testosterone talking. He's a barrister, remember, and would have done you—and WLS—a whole lot more damage than anything you could inflict on him with your fists,' she pointed out practically.

He rounded on her, his eyes glittering hotly. 'How the devil can you stay so cool about it?'

'Years of practice! I went up to Cambridge determined to do what Laura and Mother urged—to put it behind me and get on with my life.'

'So Isabel knows about this?'

'Of course. She was wonderful. So was Laura.'

Max stood looking at her in silence for a moment. 'Does anyone else know?' he asked at last.

'Sadie Morris knows about the assault, but not who did it, or about the baby. Domenico's the only one who knows the whole story. His reaction was pretty much like yours at first. But once he'd got over that he became ultra-protective instead. He still is.' Abby got up, a look in her eyes that warned Max not to touch her. She slid Luisa's ring from her finger and held it out. 'So now you know I'm not perfect, or even almost perfect, you'd better have this back.'

Max stared at it, sudden panic surging up inside him. 'What the hell are you saying, Abby?'

'Only that you're having a hard time trying to deal with my little story.' Her mouth twisted. 'Be honest, Max, you can't help wondering if little Abby with her long legs and her mini-skirt was too much of a temptation that night and got more than she bargained for.'

'Even if you were I understand why,' he said quickly. 'You'd never had a boyfriend, but you had a long-standing crush on Kent. You probably sent out signals he misunderstood.'

Abby stared at him incredulously. 'I did *not*. But there's not much point in insisting on that, because you seem more inclined to believe Marcus than me.'

'That's not true—'

'It's the way it sounds to me, Max,' she said wearily, holding out the ring. 'Take it, please.'

'Like hell I will! Are you really willing to let this man come between us?'

'*I'm* not. You're the one with the problem, Max.' She smiled bleakly. 'You said God help the man who tried to take me away from you, yet Marcus Kent has done that without lifting a finger.'

He brushed that aside. 'Were you going to tell me about the baby?'

'No.'

A pulse throbbed beside his clenched mouth. 'You don't think I had a right to know?'

'I was worried about how you'd take it. And I was right. Accepting me with all faults was a lot easier for you in theory than in practice.' Abby got up and put the ring on the small table beside him. 'Would you please go now? I'd like to get to bed. I've had rather a full day.'

Max got up, his eyes full of remorse. 'Abby, forgive me. I forgot to ask about the new job—'

'You were too taken up with your accusations.' She shrugged disdainfully. 'Since you've finally got round to asking, I enjoyed my day a whole lot more than my evening, Max. And I don't forgive you. For anything.' Abby made for the stairs, determined he shouldn't see her cry. 'Let yourself out, please.'

'Abby, wait!' Max lunged after her to catch her by the hand, but she shook him off and ran up to her room.

It was rare in Max Wingate's adult life to be at a loss. His instinct was to race after Abby, take her in his arms and convince her that he loved her so much that nothing could ever alter that. When he thought of her struggling in Kent's arms, he wanted to smash the man's teeth in, but in trying to be reasonable and understanding about it for her sake he'd made a spectacular mistake. Right now it was unlikely she'd listen to him, let alone believe him. Better to go home, sleep on it, and leave it until tomorrow to talk to her. Only sleep would be impossible when he knew damn well she was sobbing her heart out.

He leapt up the stairs and tried to open her door, but it was locked. He knocked on it and waited.

'Abby, let me in. Please.'

Silence. Now what? He could hardly break the door down. He was in enough trouble already. As he raised his hand to knock again the door opened, and Abby glared at him with swollen, bloodshot eyes.

'Sex might have been the cure for your tears, Max Wingate, but it isn't for mine, so get lost!'

And before he could open his mouth to protest she'd slammed the door on him and rammed her message home by turning the key in the lock.

As Max turned to go downstairs he found Isabel Green in the hall, looking up at him in surprise.

'Max? Abby didn't say you were coming this evening.'

He raked a despairing hand through his hair. 'The dinner ended early, so I drove over to see Abby. We had a row, and now she won't talk to me.'

The familiar topaz eyes were kind. 'Do you want to talk to me instead?'

'If you could spare a minute to listen I'd be grateful.'

'Of course. Let's go in the kitchen. I'll make some coffee, or tea, or maybe you'd like a drink?'

Max shook his head. 'Thank you, but I'm not sure I could swallow even that right now.'

'As bad as that! Let's sit down in comfort in the parlour, then.' Isabel's eyes narrowed as she spotted the glittering ring on the side table. 'Oh, dear. Abby gave that back to you?'

'Yes. But I refused to take it.'

She sighed. 'This sounds serious. You'd better sit down and tell me if there's anything I can do.'

Max told his brief tale succinctly, his eyes grim as he finished. 'I meant that whatever happened that night I understood and she wasn't to blame. But it didn't come out quite like that. God, I've made a mess of things. But I refuse to let such a small thing keep us apart, Isabel.'

'To Abby, the fact that you even suspected for a minute that she'd led Marcus Kent on is a very big thing.' Isabel looked him in the eye. 'He almost ruined her life back then. Are you going to let him do it again?'

'Hell, no!' He got to his feet. 'When Abby ran to her room, crying, I went up after her to try to put things right.'

'But she slammed the door in your face.'

'How did you know?'

'I'm a woman,' she said dryly.

'She wouldn't let me near her, but it tore me to pieces to see her cry like that. For God's sake, go up and comfort her, Isabel.'

She patted his arm consolingly as she saw him out. 'I'll try some tea and sympathy on my daughter in a moment. Meanwhile, you go home and get some sleep. Are you coming round tomorrow evening?'

He shook his head despairingly. 'I can't. My father's coming down from London.'

'Of course. We were all supposed to lunch together on Saturday.' She gave him a rueful smile. 'Right now, that doesn't seem a very likely prospect. Ring Abby tomorrow.'

'I will. In the meantime, will you give her a message?'

'Of course.'

Max looked at her steadily. 'Just tell her I love her.'

Next morning Isabel drove a very heavy-eyed Abby to Millwood House before going to school. 'I think you should have at least spoken to Max when he rang just now.'

'I don't want to talk to him. Besides, I couldn't without crying again, and I look enough of a mess already.'

'Tell the Colonel you've got a cold,' Isabel said gently. 'And if the van doesn't materialise today ring me and I'll come for you tonight.'

Abby kissed her gratefully. 'Thanks, Mother. I promise to be more cheerful by the time I get home.'

But since most of her time was spent in supervising preparations for a wedding that day, this was a difficult promise to keep. Following instructions from Mrs Ellison, Abby consulted with the caterers, cast a critical eye over the tables laid in the main hall for the wedding breakfast, and finally went to check on the flowers in the chapel which had once been the private place of worship for the owners of Millwood House. Pretty, but not her cup of tea, thought Abby. Not that it mattered any more.

Abby sat at the back of the chapel to watch the service, and then stood on the sidelines at the reception while the photographs were taken. Afterwards, she kept watch while the meal was served, but when the cake had been cut and the speeches were almost over she went back to Mrs Ellison's office to report that the bridal car was ready and waiting to take the bride and groom to the airport, and the proceedings had gone without a hitch.

'Do you fancy something like that for your own wedding, Abby?'

Abby said it was certainly a possibility. But it was no longer a probability, she thought despondently as she drove home in the dark blue van emblazoned with the gold logo of Millwood House. Maybe she was expecting too much of Max. He was a man, and human, so she could hardly blame him for his doubts. But she did, just the same. It was so *unfair*, she thought fiercely as she turned down the lane for home. She'd been so thrilled and flattered when Marcus had invited her to a concert all those years ago. And when he'd parked on the way home to kiss her goodnight she'd been thrilled and flattered by that, too. Until the romance had turned into nightmare.

When she reached Briar Cottage she sat outside for a moment, thinking back to the incident she'd tried so hard to blot from her mind. Was Max right? Was it possible that she'd unknowingly sent out the wrong signals to Marcus that night? Her eyes hardened. Even if she had, she'd paid dearly enough afterwards. And she was still paying.

When Abby went into the house Isabel sighed with relief. 'You look a lot better, darling. Take a look in the other room and you'll feel better still.'

A vast sheaf of fiery chrysanthemums made a splash of colour which lit up the room. 'Those are for me, I suppose.'

'Of course.' Isabel handed her an unopened envelope. 'This came with them.'

Abby took out the card, her teeth sunk in her bottom lip as she read the terse message: *I love you. Max.*

'Do you feel better now?' asked Isabel when Abby gave her the card.

'Not much. Marcus said I'd been a constant temptation to him as a teenager, and Max has a problem with that. So I'm beginning to think maybe I unknowingly led Marcus on and it really was my fault.'

'That is utter nonsense,' said her mother hotly. 'You always thought Rachel was the pretty one, and could never see how attractive you were yourself. Besides, even if you were a temptation, the man shouldn't have acted on it.' Her eyes flashed. 'I could have killed him with my bare hands.'

'Me too. And Laura.' Abby grinned suddenly. 'Domenico wanted to beat him up at the time, and Max wanted to last night. So one way and another Marcus is quite lucky he's still in one piece.' She jumped as the phone rang. 'You answer it. If it's Max, say I'm out.'

'No. Even for you I'm not lying.' Isabel hurried into the kitchen but shook her head at Abby as she picked up the phone. 'Hello, Lewis.'

Abby had a bath, ate some of the meal her mother cooked, and afterwards tried to interest herself in a programme on television. But because Isabel received two phone calls from friends during the evening Abby had very little success.

'You're like a cat on hot bricks,' said her mother. 'If you don't want to speak to Max why are you jumping up every time the phone rings? Besides,' she added, 'wouldn't Max ring you on your mobile?'

'Yes, of course. I'm pretty poor company tonight. Sorry.'

Isabel sighed. 'Why not get it over with? Ring Max and thank him for the flowers, then get into bed and catch up on some of the sleep you missed last night.'

'I suppose you're right.' Abby eyed her mother guiltily. 'Was Lewis asking you out earlier? Did you refuse on my account?'

'Yes, to both questions. But don't worry. I'm seeing him

tomorrow night.' Isabel smiled as she held up her face for Abby's kiss. 'Goodnight, love.'

Abby sat on the side of her bed for a long time before she could bring herself to ring Max. 'It's Abby,' she said, when his recorded voice asked her to leave a message. 'Thank you for the flowers. Regards to David. Goodbye.'

An hour passed before her phone startled her into dropping her book on the floor.

'Abby?' said Max. 'I've just got in. Dad's train was late.'

'How is he?'

'Tired and hungry, but otherwise fine. How are *you*?'

'I'm fine too.'

'Abby, about tomorrow's lunch—'

'Apologise to David, but I don't think there's much point in that now.'

'I see,' he said, after a silence which stretched her nerves to breaking point. 'He'll be deeply disappointed. He was looking forward to seeing you again.'

'As I said in my message, please give him my regards.'

He breathed in audibly. 'You're really going to let this come between us, Abby?'

Something in his tone got her on the raw. 'What "this" are we talking about? The fact that I tempted a man to rape me, that I got pregnant as a result, that I would have kept that from you if I could? Or all of the above?'

'Do you feel better after that?' he demanded roughly. 'I hope so, because I damn well don't.'

'That was the object of the exercise,' she snapped, and turned the phone off, glad she'd had the last word. She was so glad she buried her face in her pillow, soaking it with her tears until her mother's hand on her shoulder brought her upright. 'I heard from Max,' she said hoarsely.

'I know,' said Isabel. 'He rang me just now.'

'I won't speak to him,' Abby said fiercely, and blew her nose.

'He wasn't expecting you to. Max said you'd switched your phone off, so he wanted me to make sure you're all right. I knew you wouldn't be, but I'm here anyway.' Isabel smoothed the hair away from her daughter's damp face. 'He sounded terrible.'

'Good.'

'You're determined to make him suffer, then.'

'Yes.'

'I feel sorry for Max's father—not a happy weekend for him.'

'I'm sorry for David, too—but not for Max.'

Isabel sat on the edge of the bed and gave Abby a straight look. 'Listen, darling. There is nothing Max can do to take back what he said, even though his intention was to show you weren't to blame. So either you let it assume mammoth proportions as an unforgivable sin, or you put it behind you where it belongs and marry him. He's just a mortal man. You wouldn't enjoy being married to a saint—he'd probably be hopeless in bed.'

'Mother!'

Abby had been awake for quite a while when Isabel came into the room with a tray next morning.

'Breakfast,' she said inexorably. 'Eat it.'

'Yes, ma'am,' said Abby, scrambling upright.

Isabel eyed her searchingly. 'You don't look too bad, all things considered. It's a lovely day, so after breakfast have a shower to perk you up, then we'll go out for a walk.'

'Good idea. Thanks.'

When Abby arrived downstairs in jeans and a heavy white sweater, unworn since the previous winter, she heard voices in the kitchen and hesitated, tray in hand. If it was Lewis she didn't want to walk in on some private *tête-à-tête* without warning. She coughed before opening the kitchen door, then smiled in spontaneous delight when David Wingate got up to greet her. Abby dumped the tray on the table and as though it were the most natural thing in the world ran into the arms he held out. He hugged her, kissed her cheek, then put her away to look down into her face.

'Good morning, Abby. I've just been making your mother's acquaintance over some excellent coffee. How are you today?'

'I've been better,' she admitted wryly, and smiled at her mother as she removed the tray. 'I've been indulged with breakfast in bed this morning.'

'A little indulgence now and then does no harm,' said Isabel, topping up David's coffee.

'As you've probably guessed,' he said, as Abby sat down beside him, 'I'm here as emissary. For once in his life Max feels so helpless he's asked me to plead his case for him. As you know, emotionally he's had quite a bit to deal with lately. Have you told Isabel about Luisa's revelation?'

'No.' Abby gave her mother an apologetic look. 'It seemed too private to discuss without permission.'

'Then I'll explain.' David related the story in detail, including everything Luisa had said before the party. 'It makes no difference to me who actually fathered him,' he said at last. 'Max was mine from the moment I laid eyes on him. I let my wife go when she met Enzo again. But I kept my son.'

'Max said Luisa's bombshell made no difference to him, either,' said Abby. 'As far as he's concerned, you're his father, David, and that's that. Is he happy now you've sorted it out?'

A pair of wry blue eyes probed hers. 'I don't think Max will ever be happy again without *you*, Abby.'

She bit her lip. 'He hurt me.'

'I know. He wants so much to make up for that. Are you willing to let him try?'

'Where is he now?' said Isabel.

'At home in Pennington. I used his car to drive here.' David looked at her hopefully. 'Do you have a suggestion?'

'Yes. Abby, I think you should go and see Max and talk things over. And, if nothing can be done to heal the breach, come back and get on with your life.' Isabel smiled lovingly. 'You're good at that. You've done it before.'

David took Abby's hand. 'Do it for me, if not for Max.'

'In that case I can hardly say no,' she said huskily, and got up. 'Perhaps I'd better ring him.'

'No,' said Isabel decisively. 'Just turn up and surprise him. Take the Mini if you like.'

'Certainly not. Love me, love my van.'

'Good girl,' approved David. 'If all goes well, let us know and I'll drive your mother into Pennington for this lunch Max arranged.'

'Worst scenario, come back on your own and I'll put on lunch for the three of us here,' said Isabel, practical as always.

The drive to Pennington had never seemed so long. The van had been designed for durability rather than speed, and by the time Abby parked in the road in Chester Gardens she was regretting the whole thing. She locked the van, squared her shoulders, then marched up the short drive to the house and rang the bell. Max opened the door and stood transfixed, his eyes blazing with such incredulous delight Abby thawed a little as he drew her inside and closed the door.

'You came,' he said huskily. 'I didn't think you would.'

She shrugged. 'Your father and my mother make a powerful team. They thought we should talk.'

'They're absolutely right.' He paused to look down at her. 'But I can think of only one thing to say. I love you, Abby.'

'That's a very important thing,' she conceded.

'Also important, do you love me?'

Not much point in lying. 'Yes,' she admitted reluctantly.

He let out a deep breath. 'Thank God for that.'

'I wavered badly when you gave Marcus Kent the benefit of the doubt,' she said stringently.

Max took her by the hand and led her into his study. 'I wanted to rip his heart out, not give him the benefit of any doubt. But, being a man, I could also picture the effect you must have had on him. You seem unaware of your own allure now, when you're all grown up, Abigail Green, so you probably had even less idea back then. Kent obviously found you irresistible, and he also knew you had a crush on him. How had you spent the evening?'

'At one of the picnic concerts. We huddled under a blanket together.'

Max rolled his eyes. 'I rest my case! It was probably all the foreplay the man could take.'

'So you don't think I'm to blame?'

'God, no,' he said, appalled. 'He was wholly to blame, Abby. He probably still feels guilty as hell every time he lays eyes on you.'

'So why did he try to spoil things between us?'

'He still wants you, Abby.' Max drew her down on the sofa. 'Now then, Abigail Green, I'm going to say one more thing on the subject before we drop it, preferably for ever. Marcus Kent may want you, but he can't have you. You're mine.'

'Why didn't you say all that before?' she demanded.

'I tried. You slammed your door in my face.'

'What did you expect after hurting me like that?'

'I didn't mean to hurt you. And I never will again.'

'You can't promise that.'

'I promise to try.' Max took her by the shoulders and gave her a shake. 'But never tell me to get lost again.'

'I won't.' Abby smiled wryly. 'It was a very satisfying thing to say at the time, but I cried my eyes out afterwards.' She gave him a challenging look. 'You hurt me, so shouldn't you kiss me better?'

'God, yes,' he said fervently, and pulled her onto his lap, kissing her with a pent-up hunger she responded to so fever-ishly that Max leaned his forehead against hers, breathing harshly. 'I want you so much, Abby. But not just for this.'

'It's the best way to make up,' she said breathlessly. 'I gave you comfort when you needed it, but I need some now. Fair's fair.'

Max pulled her close and began kissing her with mounting heat as he undressed her, awkward in his haste because he couldn't stop kissing her to speed the process. At last he laid her naked against the sofa cushions, and Abby pulled him down to her, arms and legs around him in a welcome that dispensed with all other preliminaries as they joined together in passionate reconciliation.

After a long, deeply satisfying interval of just holding each other close in the aftermath, Abby sat up with a gasp and looked at her watch. 'Is that the time? I need to call Mother and tell her lunch is on at the Chesterton after all.'

'Tell her to bring the ring!'

Max held Abby tightly as she made the phone call, smoothing his hand down her bare back as Abby rather incoherently set their respective parents' minds at rest.

'Right,' said Max as Abby disconnected. 'Dad's a cautious driver, so we have a good half-hour to come back to earth and look respectable.'

'David said you sorted out the paternity question,' said Abby as she pulled on her clothes.

'We both agreed that it didn't matter. He's been my father and I've been his son for thirty-five years, and we're both very happy with the arrangement.' Max handed her a shoe. 'Now I have you, Dad's even happier.' He tipped her face up to his. 'Tell me I *do* have you, Abby.'

She reached up to kiss him. 'Of course you do. You're stuck with me—for keeps.'

Max grinned, his eyes laughing into hers. 'Perfect.'

Much to Colonel Granger's satisfaction, the Wingate/Green wedding was such a success it was great publicity for

Millwood House. The bride, in a trailing-sleeved ivory velvet gown with a medieval air to it, was given away with great pride by her handsome brother-in-law, Domenico Chiesa, and followed down the aisle by her niece Isabella, a beaming Botticelli angel in organza the pale gold of her curls.

'Not many brides get the competition I had to put up with yesterday,' said Abigail Wingate as her husband drove at a leisurely pace up the serpentine road to his hilltop retreat next day. 'My mother and Laura looked wonderful enough, but when your father led your mother in with Renata there was an audible gasp, according to Rachel.'

'I didn't notice. And once you came down the aisle I only had eyes for you,' Max assured her, and Abby laughed.

'I wasn't fishing, honestly!'

'You looked as though you'd stepped from a medieval tapestry. I don't know what Guinevere looked like, or even if she existed, but if she was anything like you in that dress King Arthur was a lucky man.'

'Until Lancelot arrived on the scene, anyway.' She put her hand on his knee. 'No Lancelot in our story, Max.'

'Good. Our hiccup came before the wedding.'

Abby giggled. 'Marcus in the role of hiccup—I like it.'

'What did he say when he declined the wedding invitation?'

'Due to an unavoidable appearance in court he was unable to attend. He sent us a rather nice crystal claret jug with his regrets, though. Why are you stopping here?' she added, surprised.

'This, my darling Mrs Wingate, is the bend where we first met.' Max leaned over and kissed her before driving on.

Abby gave a deep sigh of satisfaction. 'If they use blue plaques in Italy we should erect one on that bit of hillside. "Abigail and Max Wingate met here".'

'And lived happily ever after,' said Max firmly.

When they arrived at the house they found a small familiar car parked in the courtyard, and Rosa hurried out, her face wreathed in smiles, greeting them in a flood of good wishes and welcome that Max had no need to translate.

With much hand-waving and the occasional word from Max, she showed Abby the supplies stacked in the cupboards, and the dishes she'd left ready in the refrigerator to heat. After a long session of questions and answers with Max, she kissed them both and went out to her car to drive back to the Villa Falcone.

'She was asking about Gianni, of course,' said Abby, as she followed Max upstairs with some of the luggage.

'And the wedding. I told her the service was beautiful, and Renata accompanied Gianni so beautifully as he sang "Panis Angelicus" there wasn't a dry eye in the house.' Max gave her a very explicit look as they reached the master bedroom. 'To change the subject to more secular things, you may care to know, Mrs Wingate, that the very first time I mentioned the beautiful view from this room I pictured you here, sharing my bed.'

Abby sat on the edge of it, eyeing him in surprise. 'I'd never have known!'

'I'm good at hiding my feelings.' He put an arm round her as he joined her. 'At least, I was at the time. Right now you can probably read me like a book.'

'You mean you'd like a little nap?'

He nuzzled her cheek in appreciation. 'I knew there was a good reason for marrying you, darling. You understand me so well.'

'Right,' she said, and took off for the door, laughing at the look on his face. 'You have a nap while I get supper ready. Because once I get in that bed I probably won't want to get out of it until tomorrow. And right now I'm—'

'Hungry,' he said, laughing, and put his arm round her as they went downstairs. 'All right, you win. But have mercy, woman. Let's eat something we don't have to cook.'

Over a meal of soup, bread and salad, followed by slices

of the almond torte Rosa had left for them, they talked over the wedding, which Abby described with the word borrowed from her husband. 'It was just perfect,' she said as they made coffee. 'I know Gianni and Renata have to fly back tomorrow, but how long do you think Luisa will stay in Kew with David?'

'For a few days, at least—she was talking about some shopping in London before she leaves.'

'Luisa seemed very comfortable with David. Do you think they'll get back together?'

'They won't get married again. Luisa is still grieving for Enzo. But I think she and Dad will see something of each other in future. She's invited him to stay in Venice soon.'

'Good. He can call on Laura at the same time. He seemed very taken with my sister.'

'Hardly surprising.' Max grinned. 'Domenico looked as proud as punch as he escorted you down the aisle yesterday.'

'I can't get over how good baby Marco was, too. But Laura's friend Fen Dysart—beg her pardon, Mrs Tregenna now—walked him up and down in his buggy during the service until Papa took over at the reception. Marco's a very sociable baby. He seemed to enjoy the fun as much as everyone else.'

Max got up suddenly, fixing her with an imperious look. 'Right. That's it. Any more talking, Abigail Wingate, can be done in bed.'

'Yes, O master,' she said with mock docility, and he grinned and took her hand.

'Just keep saying that and you'll make a perfect wife!'

When they were in bed together, Max drew her against him with a deep, relishing sigh. 'At last! I've been thinking about this all day. Just to have you here in my arms is enough for the moment. Though probably not for long.'

Abby wriggled closer. 'Will making love be any different now we're married?'

'It was pretty spectacular last night!'

'Only to be expected. That was our wedding night. Now we're an old married couple, maybe it will be different from now on.'

Max laughed and kissed her, his hands beginning a slow, relishing exploration which caused delicious tremors in the nude, slender body pressed close to his. 'Now you've got the hang of it, I guarantee that it will get better. And if it isn't we've got the rest of our lives to practise until it's—'

'Perfect,' she finished for him, laughing.

A long time later, when they lay almost asleep in each other's arms, Abby raised her head. 'I've got an idea.'

Max nuzzled her neck. 'Tell me it doesn't involve getting out of this bed,' he said drowsily.

'Wake up and listen. How do you feel about having everyone to our house for Christmas dinner?'

He reached out to switch on the light, shaking his head as he looked down into her flushed face. 'We've just had a fore-taste of paradise together—despite being an old married couple—and all you can think about is food?'

Abby gave him a punch on the arm. 'Be serious. I think it would be wonderful to get the whole family together, yours and mine, for our first Christmas together. Can we?'

He smoothed his cheek against her hair. 'How can I refuse when you said something so important just now?'

'All of it was important. Which bit do you mean?'

'You referred to it as our house, which means you feel you belong there.'

'Of course I belong there. It's where you are.'

Max gave a deep sigh and pulled her close. 'I love you, Abby.'

'I love you, too.' She wriggled closer. 'Max?'

'Yes, darling?'

'I don't think we've got it quite right yet. And due to my slow start in this kind of thing I've got a lot to make up.'

He laughed and kissed her, smoothing a hand down her back. 'You want to practise some more?'

'If that's all right with you?'

'It's a lot more than all right,' he assured her, his voice uneven as his bride resorted to caresses she was growing more skilled at every time they made love.

'How would you describe it, then?' she demanded.

'Perfect,' said Max.

And it was.

researching the cure

The facts you need to know:

- Breast cancer is the commonest form of cancer in the United Kingdom. **One woman in nine** will develop the disease during her lifetime.

- Each year around **41,000** women and approximately **300** men are diagnosed with breast cancer and around **13,000** women and **90** men will die from the disease.

- 80% of all breast cancers occur in post-menopausal women and approximately 8,200 pre-menopausal women are diagnosed with the disease each year.

- However, survival rates are improving, with on average 77.5% of women diagnosed between 1996 and 1999 still alive five years later, compared to 72.8% for women diagnosed between 1991 and 1996.

Breast Cancer Campaign is the only charity that specialises in funding independent breast cancer research throughout the UK. It aims to find the cure for breast cancer by funding research which looks at improving diagnosis and treatment of breast cancer, better understanding how it develops and ultimately either curing the disease or preventing it.

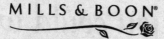

MILLS & BOON®

All you could want for Christmas!

Meet handsome and seductive men under the mistletoe, escape to the world of Regency romance or simply relax by the fire with a heartwarming tale by one of our bestselling authors. These special stories will fill your holiday with Christmas sparkle!

On sale 6th October 2006

On sale 20th October 2006

4 FREE

BOOKS AND A SURPRISE GIFT!

We would like to take this opportunity to thank you for reading this Mills & Boon® book by offering you the chance to take FOUR more specially selected titles from the Modern Romance™ series absolutely FREE! We're also making this offer to introduce you to the benefits of the Mills & Boon® Reader Service™—

- ★ **FREE home delivery**
- ★ **FREE gifts and competitions**
- ★ **FREE monthly Newsletter**
- ★ **Exclusive Reader Service offers**
- ★ **Books available before they're in the shops**

Accepting these FREE books and gift places you under no obligation to buy, you may cancel at any time, even after receiving your free shipment. Simply complete your details below and return the entire page to the address below. You don't even need a stamp!

YES! Please send me 4 free Modern Romance books and a surprise gift. I understand that unless you hear from me, I will receive 6 superb new titles every month for just £2.80 each, postage and packing free. I am under no obligation to purchase any books and may cancel my subscription at any time. The free books and gift will be mine to keep in any case.

P6ZED

Ms/Mrs/Miss/Mr ....Initials ....

BLOCK CAPITALS PLEASE

Surname ....

Address ....

....

....Postcode...............................

Send this whole page to:
UK: FREEPOST CN81, Croydon, CR9 3WZ